LIFESAVER

Janice Bartlett

A KISMET® Romance

METEOR PUBLISHING CORPORATION
Bensalem, Pennsylvania

JANICE BARTLETT

Janice has a B.A. in history and a master's degree in librarianship. She gave up being a public librarian to write full time. Now the author of twenty-two books, including a picture book and six novels for young adults, Janice lives north of Seattle, Washington, with her two daughters, five cats and one dog. She loves to garden and write.

Other books by Janice Bartlett:

ONE

Megan Lovell hesitated at the stop sign, then finally turned her small red Civic to the right, onto the lake road. The highway would be faster, but the evening was too beautiful to waste.

Peach and pink and golden, the sky glowed like a stained-glass window above the pine- and fir-cloaked ridge beyond the lake. But for the plumes of some power boats out in the middle, the water was uncannily still, reflecting the sky and the deep purple shadows that moved down the valley, bringing dusk here sooner than it came to the world beyond. It was a display that made her wish she had her camera.

Lights were on in the cluster of waterfront cottages she passed as people cleaned up after dinner, got the children ready for bed, settled down with a book. Already the gaudy tint had faded, softened, and the ridge was black. The water still shone like a mirror, but it would be dark soon, too.

Megan left the cottages behind as the narrow road rose to follow an empty cove of the lake. Sheer granite rocks sloped down into the water. A few small twisted firs and hemlock clung to cracks. On impulse she steered the car into a dirt turnoff, then parked it and climbed out. She found a comfortable rock to sit on as she watched the show. The colors were incredible, incandescent and yet soft and subtle like the merest wash in a watercolor, with the ridge forming a black silhouette. The sight tightened her throat. It was moments like this, utterly peaceful and achingly beautiful, that made living here worth the price of isolation.

The low coughing sound of a boat engine broke the stillness, coming from beyond the point. When it came in sight, the big white powerboat was moving slowly, at about trolling speed, cutting a silver wake in the still water, making tiny waves slap at the rock walls of the cove. Megan couldn't see any fishing poles, but the boat was familiar: she was fairly certain it was rented from the marina. The engine was turned off as the boat drifted into the large, deserted cove. Megan watched with idle curiosity, wondering if the boaters were having engine trouble, or simply enjoying the evening as she was. She doubted they could see her or the road above, and even they were indistinct in the increasing shadows.

In fact, it was time to go. She was suddenly aware of how hungry she was, and how tired. The heat of a new sunburn singed her shoulders and cheekbones and her eyes felt the strain of a day spent staring at water reflecting the sun's brilliance. From fall to spring Megan taught kindergarten in the small local school, but from the time she'd quit competitive swimming she had spent summers lifeguarding at the public beach. The county had been good about giving her time off to do endorsements; in return, she'd been something of a tourist attraction for the first few years. She had worked at the beach for six years now and as the manager for the last four.

"You ought to be sick of the lake," she said aloud. But somehow Megan knew that she wasn't and never would be. Devil's Lake was home. If she sometimes felt she had to pay a price for the right to belong here, it was a belief she kept to herself.

Megan was about to slide off her boulder and retreat to her car when motion out on the boat arrested her attention. Two men were standing. She *thought* they were men. The boat rocked as they seemed to be lifting something bulky, struggling to get it over the gunwale. Then the long dark shape fell, raising a small splash as it hit, sending ripples to shiver over the mirrorlike surface of the lake. For a second the shape seemed to move, to struggle, although that might have been an illusion. For then, slowly, it slipped beneath the water in quiet surrender.

Megan's mouth was open, a cry trapped in her throat. For a moment stillness reigned as the men stared down at the water and she tried to comprehend what she had seen. Already the ripples were fading, the dark shape gone as if it had never been. By the time the boat engine roared harshly to life, Megan had jumped from the rock and was running.

Over the guardrail, sliding down a slab of granite, desperately pushing past small firs. The soles of her canvas tennis shoes slipped and she fell to her knees, but she didn't even notice the pain. The rocky point that protected the cove sloped downhill, not wide enough to have been built on, but a faint trail showed that fishermen or teenagers out for a skinny dip sometimes came this way. Megan let her feet find their own path, faster than was safe. Her eyes were glued to the spot where the ripples had begun. The boat had sprung away, the powerful engine at full throttle, and in a wide curve disappeared out into the open lake.

Stumbling to a stop where the point dropped into the deep, cold water, Megan kicked off her shoes, ripped off her jeans. She hadn't even stopped to think. A lifeguard didn't, when someone was drowning. Knowing it was probably futile, still she was about to dive in when something white broke the surface of the water out in the middle of the cove. A splash, an arm reaching for the help that wasn't there. Another splash. That much she could see. The struggle was weak, desperate. She hit the water, scarcely aware of the shock from the cold. Head down, she sprinted, faster than she had ever gone back in her racing days. She didn't want to take her eyes off the victim, but there was too far to go. Speed was more important.

Several times she lifted her head, focused just long enough to be sure she was aiming in the right direction. Near the end she swam with her head up, her crawl stroke choppy but fast. Ahead, the struggles diminished. *Hold on*, Megan screamed silently. *Hold on.* For a second she lost sight, as if the lake had won, but then a dark head reappeared, a feeble splash.

It was a man, floating on his back, eyes closed, water sliding over his face. He looked dead.

Megan slipped up behind him, cupped his chin and swiftly tucked her other arm over his chest, locking his long body against her hip. She was prepared when he fought briefly, though she was submerged by his weight and strength. When he collapsed into quiescence again, Megan shook the water from her face and said urgently, "It's okay. I'm going to help you. Can you hear me? Just relax."

For a second he stirred and she tightened her grasp, but then she heard a hoarse voice. "Can't swim."

"It's okay," she said again, her legs opening and closing in a powerful scissor kick. He was heavy, too heavy for her. She had to snatch breaths as water rolled over her face. Darkness was closing with frightening suddenness. It was a miracle that she had seen him thrown overboard. Ten minutes later she wouldn't have. If only she could swim for the nearest shore, but the rock slabs dropping into the cove were too steep. Only at the tip of the point would she be able to pull him out. Already she was exhausted.

She had told him a lie. It wasn't okay. They wouldn't make it. Not like this. If he couldn't help . . . But she refused to think about it. Stopping, Megan treaded water, supporting his head and shoulders. She could hear herself breathing in desperate gasps.

"I need your help," she said forcefully. "Are you listening?"

An eternity seemed to pass, and then his head nodded, rocking against her breast.

"I need you to float on your back, with your hands on my shoulders. You have to keep your arms stiff. Can you do that?"

Again the pause, the achingly slow response. Again a nod. She wondered if his thoughts were moving as slowly.

As he floated free, she kept her hand beneath his neck, making sure he didn't swallow water. They changed position, his hands groping blindly before finding her shoulders to grasp with frightening strength.

For just an instant his eyes opened. She could tell they were light colored, his face was so close to hers. In their glazed depths she saw the battle he fought to hold on. Her lips moved to reassure him again, but the words died as his eyes closed.

She used the strong breaststroke that had won her a spot on the U.S. Olympic team. Their passage was utterly quiet. Time seemed to have begun and ended. It was a nightmare, her fear a part of the gathering dusk and the bone-deep cold of the water. What if her strength gave out? Would she have the courage to let him go, watch him slip into the dark tomb below?

The sound of a car passing on the lake road came to her, then the muted call of an owl. She wondered if the man might have died, if his fingers might be clenching her in a death grip. Then the rasp of a harsh breath stilled that fear.

The point lay just ahead, like the back of a great beast rising out of the lake. Megan strained her eyes to see, praying that she wouldn't ram his head against a rock. Almost there, she thought. Almost there. Dark water slapped over the man's face and he coughed weakly. He must have a concussion at least, she thought.

Suddenly she became aware of the twin beams of headlights on the road above, playing over the trees, the rocks, her car. She imagined the driver, maybe even someone she knew, admiring the last hint of color above the ridge, never guessing at the drama below in the dusk-shrouded cove. Only then, just past the turnoff, there was a quick flicker of brake lights, a hesitation. Oh, God, she thought in fresh panic, like a hunted animal. What if they had come back in a car? It would be so easy for them to check the shore. There was nowhere to hide. Beneath the water might still be a refuge for her, but for him . . . impossible.

But then the car went on. Perhaps the driver had braked for a curve, or had hesitated as he glanced at her Honda, wondering if somebody might need help. Well, she needed help all right, but the road and any passing drivers were beyond her reach.

"We're here," she said loudly, in a voice that cracked. "You have to let go of me now."

One finger at a time, he obeyed. Megan slipped under him, hugging him about the chest again as she felt for the rocks ahead with her free hand. There. A scrape against her fingertips. Too steep. She turned to edge along the shore. Her knee skinned against a rock as she scissor-kicked, but the sting scarcely registered.

Suddenly the rock was flat and she braced herself with her hand, pulling the weight of two bodies in. Laying his head on the rock, she crawled out, grabbed him under the arms, and struggled to pull him higher out of the water. He was impossibly heavy, dead weight. She was shaking all over from cold and fear and exhaustion. But they had made it, she realized; she could safely let him go. At last she crumpled beside him, half in, half out of the water.

Megan began to think again when a spasm shook him. Could she go for help? She was afraid to leave him alone. And afraid to stop any car that passed. She had no idea what the men in the boat had looked like. What if she led death right to him, after she had fought so hard for his life?

It was the first time she had ever rescued anybody away from the beach, with its network of other lifeguards and a telephone that summoned an ambulance within ten minutes. At the beach they would have strapped this man to a backboard because of his head injury. But as another car drove slowly by on the road above, Megan had become increasingly conscious of their vulnerability. He was not a victim of an accident; somebody had tried to murder this man. The two men on the boat would not be happy to discover they had failed.

Megan sighed and pushed herself to a sitting position. Her shakes had eased, only to be replaced by shivers. The elevation was high enough here that nights were always cool, and the water in the deep, glacially formed lake never warmed above frigid.

She reached out a hand to touch his shoulder and he groaned.

"Can you hear me?" She was almost whispering, aware of the increasing darkness around them. "Do you think you can walk?"

Silence, then he said in a thick voice, "Walk?" There was a pause, during which she could sense his struggle to understand. "Yeah," he said finally. "God, I have a headache."

"I can go for help," Megan said. "If . . . if you'll be safe here."

A few seconds passed. "No." He rolled toward her, another groan torn from his throat. "Help me up."

Somehow she got him to his feet, although her legs were shaking again before they had taken even a step. He was taller, heavier, and when he stumbled she had to wrap both arms around his waist to keep them from falling. Stones cut into her bare feet and she wished she had taken the time to find her clothes. Her wet T-shirt and underwear didn't provide any protection. But it was too late now. At least he wore shoes along with sodden jeans and some kind of thin shirt that clung to the hard muscles of his chest and arms.

In the water she had thought it was a nightmare, but this was worse, far worse. The rocks she had so heedlessly slid down had to be laboriously climbed. Their feet slipped, his weight nearly crumpling her. The arm that lay across her shoulders felt like an iron bar, one that in normal circumstances she could never have lifted. Perhaps she had become numb, because she kept putting one bleeding foot in front of the other, kept hoisting and dragging, holding him up when he staggered, murmuring directions and encouragement.

"Up a little here. Watch out for that tree. Come on, we're almost there. We're making it."

Unbelievably, they were. They had. The ground was level, the car just ahead. They went around the end of the guardrail, instead of trying to climb over it. Across the gravel turn-out. He had leaned heavily against the car as she reached for the door handle when a horrifying thought hit her.

"My keys. Oh, my God!"

Had she put them in the pocket of her jeans? She couldn't remember. When she wrenched open the door and the small roof light came on, illuminating the key still dangling from the ignition, Megan sagged with the most overwhelming relief she had ever felt. She could have made it back down there, of course she could, but she wasn't sure how. Thank heaven for her carelessness.

"A car's coming." His voice still sounded thick, strained, but there was alarm in it.

"Get in," she said. "Hurry." She almost pushed him as he fell in, then slammed the door and ran to her own side. They had both slumped low in their seats by the time the headlights flashed over her Civic. Megan didn't breathe until the other car had passed, the sound of the engine diminishing.

Her hand trembled as she reached for the key and turned it. The engine sprang instantly to life. Megan glanced at her passenger, expecting to see his eyes closed, only to find him watching her. She was suddenly aware of his presence in a new and slightly frightening way. He had been strong enough to make it this far, when most men would have died. In the dim light from the dashboard she could see that he was big, broad-shouldered, with a face made harsh by pain. Water-darkened hair was plastered against his skull. There was something in his eyes, a wariness, that made her wary in turn. Ordinary people were not knocked unconscious and thrown overboard from a boat.

"Who are you?" he said. "Where are you taking me?"

She swallowed. "I'm Megan Lovell. I . . . I'm in charge of the public beach. I was on my way home and . . ." She stopped, bit her lip. "I'm taking you to the hospital."

She could feel his tension in the silence that followed, but suddenly he exhaled and let his head fall back against the seat's headrest. His eyes had closed. "Okay," he said in a voice that had become more slurred. "But don't tell them . . . Hell. That doesn't make sense."

"I don't understand. What doesn't make sense?" Megan put the small car in gear. It lurched when she pressed with her bare foot on the accelerator, but after a brief crunch of gravel they were on the road, heading toward town. Only darkness showed in the rearview mirror. For the first time in what seemed an eternity, she began to feel safe.

He didn't answer her directly. "What did you see?"

She told the truth. "I saw two men throw you out of the boat."

He sounded even more distant, as though every word was an effort. "Did you see . . . them?"

"You mean, to identify? No. But surely you did."

He didn't answer. When she tore her gaze from the road, it was to discover that he had slid sideways, his head now resting against the door. He looked as though he were asleep, but she knew better. Even in the darkness she saw the blood that dripped down his forehead.

Praying under her breath, Megan stamped down harder on the accelerator and the small car leaped eagerly into the curves. What if he was paralyzed because she had made him walk? What if he died? She didn't even know his name.

The medical clinic that maintained a few hospital beds was mercifully on this side of town. She pulled right up to the brightly lit emergency entrance.

Even before she had gotten out of the car, a nurse had appeared, taken in the man's condition with one glance, and turned to snap orders at an attendant who had started to follow her out. With relief Megan recognized the nurse. She'd known Pam since third grade. Suddenly superfluous, Megan hunched her shoulders, for the first time conscious of the wet T-shirt and panties that had molded themselves into a second skin. Within minutes, her passenger was on a gurney, blood pressure being checked as he was wheeled away.

When the nurse reappeared, she said, "What happened?"

"I found him drowning in the lake," Megan said acerbically. She pulled the T-shirt away from her breasts. "What's it look like?"

Her friend raised a brow, looked Megan over from her dripping hair to her bare legs, then said, "Good Lord, your feet! Stay there. No, don't move."

Megan found herself stuffed into a wheelchair with her feet immersed in a basin of something nasty that stung. The small blonde nurse swabbed antispetic on Megan's skinned knee and then taped a gauze bandage on it.

"Why didn't you call an ambulance?"

"Because it didn't happen at the beach." Megan hesitated only for a second. "Pam, some men dropped him out in the lake. Unconscious. I think you'd better call the police."

Her friend sank back on her heels, staring at Megan. "Are you sure?" She shook her head. "Never mind, you can explain it to them."

While she waited for somebody to arrive from the sheriff's office, Megan accepted the offer of a towel and a pair of sacky green scrub pants with a drawcord waist and a matching top. Looking down at herself in the new ensemble, she wrinkled her nose. Oh, well. At least she wasn't the next thing to naked.

Megan knew almost everyone in the small town, so it was no surprise to her that the deputy who showed up happened to be the father of a boy she'd had a crush on in junior high.

She greeted him with relief. "Mr. Tevis. Or should I say, Officer?"

"Pete's fine." The bony face below the graying

crewcut quirked into a smile. "Unless the uniform scares you off."

"No, I'm much too glad to see you." Behind the deputy, Pam had emerged from the emergency room looking preoccupied. Megan said quickly, "Is he . . . all right?"

"Still unconscious. Of course he has a concussion, so that's not surprising. Did he talk to you?"

Megan nodded. "His voice was slurred, but he seemed . . . well, rational."

Pam disappeared again. Pete Tevis pulled a plastic chair up in front of Megan. His graying brows rose a little at the sight of the pinkish solution in which her feet were immersed. "Blood?"

"I was barefoot."

"Okay, what's the story?"

She told him, as matter-of-factly as possible. He made notes on his clipboard, then leaned back to look at her. "You're sure the boat came from the marina?"

"I can't be positive, but I'm reasonably sure."

Without another word he stood and went behind the desk to the telephone. She couldn't quite hear his end of the conversation but assumed he had called Joe Carlson at the marina. When Pete came back, he was frowning. "A couple of strangers did rent a boat late this afternoon. They've returned it and gone. I'll follow up on the information they put on the rental form, but it may be a pack of lies. And, of course, half the boats went out today. May be a different pair altogether we're looking for."

Megan waited.

"You know anything about this fella you pulled out of the water? Look familiar?"

He wasn't the kind of man you forgot. Megan

shook her head. "I've never seen him before. I don't know all the summer crowd, though. He didn't tell me his name."

"Pam says there's no wallet in his pocket." Looking thoughtful, he ran a hand over his crewcut. "Well, I imagine he'll be able to tell me the whole story soon enough. I wouldn't mind having a chat with our two strangers who took a trip down the lake, though." He levered his long length up from the hard chair. "Well, I'll get on with it. And you should be heading on home, drying your hair and having a hot cup of tea. You can feel pretty good about what you did."

"Thanks." She smiled wryly. "I'll feel better when I know he's going to be okay."

Pete shrugged. "If he was tough enough to make it out of the lake and then walk up to the road, I don't think you need to worry. He's too stubborn to die."

Megan remembered the iron determination on the man's face, the strength that had kept him walking when his head must have felt like the aftereffects of a stick of dynamite. And maybe more astonishing, the will that had allowed him to give her his trust out in the water, when most people would have been too panicked to think rationally.

But she also remembered her first sight of him, when he had looked dead. And in the car, when his hard face had gone slack and blood had trickled over his cheek. Trying to hide her shiver, she forced a smile.

"Thanks, Pete."

With a thumb's-up, he departed, and she withdrew her feet from the basin. They were about the color of a fish's belly and wrinkled up like two raisins. A couple of the cuts welled some fresh blood as she inspected them, but Pam reappeared to patch her up, adding a pair of hospital slippers.

"Stay off your feet, okay?"

"I'll try," Megan promised. "Will you let me know when he wakes up?"

"Go home," the petite blond said firmly. "I'll call."

Megan wanted to see him again before she left, but it sounded absurd to ask. She had done all she could for him. She didn't know him; she might not even like him. She simply felt proprietary, as she might have toward a stray dog she had rescued.

But as she allowed herself to be wheeled toward the door, Megan felt as though she were deserting him.

The hospital was only five minutes from her home, a small beach cottage that was cold and dark. After letting herself in, Megan fed Zachary, her golden retriever, who had been patiently waiting on the front doorstep, then built a fire in the cast-iron wood stove. Nothing in her cupboards looked very inspiring to eat, but she finally settled for a grilled cheese sandwich. Afterward she curled up on the shabby couch under an afghan, hot cocoa beside her and a book in her hand. But somehow she felt too restless to read. If only the television reception were better; she could have used something mindless and entertaining. But without a satellite dish, TV was impossible.

When the telephone rang at nearly eleven o'clock, she snatched it up before the second ring. "Hello?"

It was Pam. "I knew I'd catch you up. Listen, how're your feet?"

"Okay," Megan said impatiently. "How is he?"

"Conscious but fuzzy. I'm not sure he remembers what happened."

Was that why he'd asked if she had seen the men? Because he didn't remember them? But Megan didn't quite believe that. He had known he wasn't safe, even once they reached the car. And the wariness in his eyes didn't fit with the picture of a confused victim who had no idea what had happened to him. Of course, he had lapsed into unconsciousness again. If he had forgotten the men, the blow on his head, had he forgotten her as well?

"He wanted to see you," the nurse continued.

Inexplicably, her heart leaped. "You mean, he asked for me by name?"

"No . . ." But Pam drew the word out, sounding uncertain. "At least, I don't think so. Did he know your name? I'm pretty sure I told him about you, and that's when he said he'd like to thank you."

Why did she feel so terribly let down? Megan wondered in dismay. Had she wanted him, a complete stranger, to *need* her? Maybe it was natural to have trouble letting go after you had saved somebody's life.

"Just let me get dressed and I'll . . ."

"Absolutely not," Pam said bluntly. "You can see him in the morning, but not before. We're keeping him under observation. And you have no business walking around on those feet."

"Those feet happen to be the only ones I own," Megan pointed out tartly. Pam always had been bossy, even as a child.

'And you don't have the option of trading them in for new ones," Pam agreed. "I'm going home in a few minutes, but I'll make sure you're expected tomorrow." A click, and she was gone.

Megan slowly hung up the phone. She should have been reassured. Instead, she felt more restless than ever. She wished she had thought to ask what Pete Tevis had found out, if anything. But probably Pam wouldn't have known.

Maybe she should call her mother. No, it was too late. In the morning, then. At last, reluctantly, she went to bed, for what good that did her.

Her mind replayed the rescue over and over. Each time, it seemed more impossible, more frightening. If she had stopped to think, would she have been so quick to dive in? If he had really struggled, had fought her with the mindless fear many drowning victims display, she could well have died out there in the dark water.

When she fell asleep at last, it was to lose herself in a strange, frustrating dream. She was on the starting blocks, every muscle in her body quivering with tension and eagerness. She knew somehow that it was the Olympic games, even though she wasn't conscious of other competitors or officials. But when she dove, the water was dark and cold and all of a sudden she was aware that something more important than a medal was at stake. But the race was endless; she couldn't see, just swam on and on in the darkness, never hitting the wall, never knowing what she pursued. Or what pursued her.

She didn't think, the next morning, that the dream race had ever ended. What did that mean? That the rescue wasn't the end, either? That the killers would be back?

But it wasn't her problem. It was his. Surely he would know *why* somebody wanted him dead, and could do something about it. She would go see him, accept his thanks, and wish him well. He was a stranger whom she would never see again.

Megan called the clinic first, then her mother. Mrs. Lovell listened in silence to Megan's story, then said quietly, "Part of me is glad you were there. For his sake."

"And the other part?"

"Wishes you had come straight home and never seen anything."

"I don't understand," she said, perplexed.

"Megan, hasn't it occurred to you that when those men find out he was rescued, they're going to know that you *saw* them? They won't like that."

"But I didn't see them!" Megan protested. "Not close enough to identify."

"Are they going to take that chance?"

She was silent for a moment. "You're scaring me," she said at last.

"I guess I meant to." Her mother's voice softened. "Just . . . be careful, will you? Until Pete figures out what's going on?"

"I'll be careful," Megan promised. "And I'll make sure that everybody knows I can't identify them. Okay?"

"Okay," Mrs. Lovell agreed. "Do you work today?"

"Are you kidding? It's Sunday. We'll be mobbed."

"Well . . . Have a good day then. Why don't you have breakfast with us tomorrow morning? We haven't seen much of you for a while".

"That sounds good, Mom. See you then."

She could have lived without that conversation, Megan thought as she dropped the receiver in the cradle. Trust her mother to worry. Only, she might be right this time.

Was that what her dream had been trying to tell her? Megan wondered. That it might not be over for her, either? That in interfering she had put herself in danger as well?

"That's ridiculous," Megan said aloud. At the sound of her voice, Zachary leaped up eagerly. "No, we're not going anywhere. At least, you're not. No, you have to stay, Zachary. Stay."

Disappointed, the big dog flopped back down. Hobbling, Megan collected her suntan lotion and towels, the lunch she'd made the night before and a book, in case she had a slow moment. Fat chance. Standing in front of the mirror, she brushed her thick, dark hair into a braid to keep it out of her face.

Ten minutes later, she pulled up in front of the clinic. She was apparently expected, so the nurse on duty let her go right in. At least she hoped it was because she was expected. Otherwise, how safe would he be here?

Megan hesitated outside the room, then took a deep breath and knocked on the door. She was inexplicably nervous. When a deep, gravelly voice said, "Come in," she opened it.

The head of the hospital bed was raised to its maximum height so that he sat up, the covers pulled loosely to his waist. Above that, his chest and shoulders were bare. He was beautifully built, with long, sleek muscles and smooth, tanned skin. But what shocked Megan was the angry scar that slanted across his upper abdomen. It didn't look very old. Clearly, this near drowning wasn't the first time he had come close to death.

At last she lifted her gaze to his face, meeting his gray eyes. He was watching her with an awareness that tightened her stomach, as though he knew what she was thinking, knew *her*, on an altogether too intimate level. His appraisal wasn't sexual in nature; it was more personal than that. Yet there was a sort of hunger to it, as though he had been waiting for hours just to see her.

Megan shifted uneasily. "Uh, hi. I'm Megan Lovell."

His voice was a little rough, like sandpaper. "I know."

"I just wanted to find out how you were feeling. Does your head hurt?"

"Like the devil." He gave a crooked smile. "That's apropos, isn't it? How the hell did your lake get a name like that?"

"It's very cold, and very deep. The Indians had stories about it. They thought something lived here, down in those depths. Maybe it did, once upon a time. At any rate, they avoided it. Devil's Lake is a rough translation of their name for it."

"I came damned close to meeting the devil face-to-face," he said wryly.

She met his gaze. "I think you had already met the devil, in his human form."

His gray eyes narrowed, seemed to search hers. "What about you? Did you meet the devil, too?"

She drew back a little from his intensity. "You asked me that last night. If I had seen them. Does it matter?"

"I don't know. I hope you didn't."

"If I hadn't seen them at all, you'd be dead."

The intensity seemed suddenly to drain out of him, leaving him looking tired. "Yeah." His half-smile was rueful. "You had the guts to put your life on the line for a total stranger's, and I haven't even thanked you, have I?''

"You don't have to. Really. It wasn't a big deal. I'm just glad . . .''

"I must outweigh you by sixty pounds," he said roughly.

"I didn't know that, when I dove in," Megan admitted. "But I've been a lifeguard for years. I knew what I was doing. Well, sort of. To tell you the truth, I just . . . reacted. I'm not sure that's being brave. Some people would call it stupid.''

His slow smile transformed his hard face, deepening the creases that were carved from nose to mouth. "You can call it whatever you want. Most people don't react that way.''

She shrugged uncomfortably. "It's over. I don't want you to feel . . .''

He made a noncommittal noise, then patted the bed beside him. "Will you sit down? Talk to me for a few minutes?''

"Uh . . . sure. Why not?'' But she had no intention of sitting on the bed. Instead, she pulled a chair over from beside the window. As she sat down, his mouth quirked with faint amusement.

When neither spoke immediately, the silence felt awkward. "You know, nobody has even told me your name," Megan said abruptly.

He looked disconcerted, seeming to hesitate. "Ross," he said at last. "Ross McKenzie. My friends call me Mac.''

Again they sat looking at each other, wordless. Megan tried to make him fit with her mental picture of the man she had rescued. She had known, in the back of her mind, that he might be attractive, even handsome, that he had a distinctive face. She had unhesitatingly told Pete Tevis that she would have known if she'd ever seen him before. She'd been right.

He had strong cheekbones, a patrician nose, a hard mouth that was still sensuous. His dark blond hair was a little long, curling on his neck and above the white bandage. The shadow of a beard showed that he hadn't shaved today, and it made him look rakish, even dangerous. Appearances were all too often deceptive; in his case, she had a feeling they were accurate.

She wanted to ask how he had come by the scar. Instead, in a polite voice, she inquired, "Do you live around here?"

"Temporarily. I've been doing some construction work. For Jim Kellerman."

"Oh. I don't think I've ever seen you."

"Or I you."

Another pause as they eyed each other. They weren't getting anywhere, Megan thought. So she said straight out, "Do you remember what happened?"

He didn't move a muscle or change his expression, yet suddenly she sensed his withdrawal. "Only hazily," he said. "I remember that I was going to take a look at a house down the lake. Give 'em a bid for an addition. After that . . ." He shrugged. "The cold water's the next thing I remember."

Megan watched him intently. "And you don't know *why* . . . ?"

"It's not the kind of thing you'd forget."

That didn't exactly answer her question. Or perhaps, in a way, it did.

"I'd better let you rest," she said, reaching for her purse. "I'm glad you're recovering, Mr. McKenzie."

He held out one hand, touched her cheek lightly. "I owe you a life for a life now."

The purse forgotten, Megan stared at him, still feeling his touch though his hand lay back at his side. "Don't be ridiculous. That sounds so . . . melodramatic. It's my job. I've pulled other people in. You don't have to . . ."

"A rule's a rule." He wasn't even smiling. "You save a life, it belongs to you. So what are you going to do with mine?"

TWO

He wished it were a joke. He'd intended to say it lightly, except that on some level he was entirely serious. She had risked her own life to save his, and the danger to her wasn't past. What he ought to do was walk away, start over in another town with another name. But if he did that, it would leave her defenseless. She'd *seen* him thrown from the boat. And that made her a threat to the men who'd tried to kill him.

He watched the shock in Megan Lovell's vivid blue eyes, then somberly, the effort she made to hide it.

After a moment, she even managed a smile. "I'll let you handle your life. Just use it well, okay?"

Frustration gripped him. He felt trapped in this sterile hospital room. "Has it occurred to you that . . ."

"Those men won't be happy to know that I saw them," she finished for him. "My mother has already been kind enough to point that out to me. One mother is enough, thanks anyway."

He raised a brow, cursed his pounding head. "Do I remind you of your mother?"

Her gaze flicked to the scar on his stomach, then back to his face. "Of course not. As long as you don't fuss."

Grimly he held those astonishing eyes with his own. "There's a time for fussing."

"I refuse to become afraid of shadows," she said, the tilt of her chin defiant. "There is no reason for them to regard me as a threat. It was dusk. I couldn't even tell you what color hair either of them had! They were just . . . figures. If they ask around town, that's what they'll hear, that I couldn't identify them. If either of us is in danger, Mr. McKenzie, it's you."

"I'm well aware of that," he said. "But since I don't have the faintest idea *why*, that makes it a little tough to act."

Her expression was frankly disbelieving, but all she said was, "If I were you, I think I'd go back wherever I came from. You have nothing to hold you here . . ."

"I have you," he said softly.

She was blunt. "No, you don't. I don't need—or want—anything from you. What I did for you, I'd have done for anyone. I don't expect any payment."

He ignored that. "Maybe you should find an excuse to disappear for a while, too. If you're gone, they're not going to hunt too hard for you."

She actually laughed. "Mr. McKenzie . . ."

He felt an unaccustomed wrench of irritation and interrupted. "Mac."

"I have a job and family and friends. This is my home. I'm not going to toss my whole life aside for weeks or months, like some book I'm not in the mood for. 'Oh, by the way, Mom, don't call me,

I'll call you. Maybe.' " She shook her head and her dark braid flopped against her shoulder. "No. Home is where I'm safest."

He gritted his teeth. "Damn it . . ."

"Goodbye, Mr. McKenzie." With that she was gone.

He stared broodingly after her, not really seeing the starkness of the hospital room. His head felt like it had the time he'd been trampled by a steer in a rodeo. He hadn't lied to her altogether; events *were* a little hazy in his mind.

But he remembered her from the first instant, when he had thought she was a mermaid he had somehow conjured from his dreams. Dark hair floating about her in the water, unfathomable eyes, arms that had held him as tightly as a mother afraid of losing her child. He had been dying, losing himself in a kaleidoscope of memories and regret that had begun to fade into darkness. And then she'd appeared, demanding his trust. That bond was not easily shaken now.

But already the part of him that had learned early not to trust was doubting. His memory had more than once kept him alive when other men would have died. And that memory told him he'd seen her face before.

Not that she was beautiful. Her face was too strong, her eyes too cool. The dark slash of brows was balanced by a stubborn chin. In between she had a small, straight nose, a scattering of freckles, and an unexpectedly soft, generous mouth. Her hair was the color of dark Belgian chocolate, glossy and thick. Today she had worn it in a fat braid down her back. Slim, she had the narrow hips, long legs, and wide shoulders of an athlete. He hadn't been thinking about her sexuality—or his—but he'd noticed her body, all right. It was her eyes, though, that made her unforgettable.

He could swear he had never met her. But, damn it, he *had* seen her. He knew he had. It tugged at the edge of his mind, he could almost remember. A long time ago, he thought, and something was different about her. The woman—no, girl—he saw was younger, more vulnerable. But definitely *her*. And that made him nervous. Who the hell was she? Someone's sister, someone's daughter? Or was he being paranoid? Maybe he'd only seen her picture in a magazine, passed her in the mall one day!

He wanted it to be chance that he knew her. He wanted that so badly, it made him wary.

He'd been a fool already to take the two strangers at face value, even though the chances of Saldivar finding him here had seemed slim. One minute he'd been enjoying the boat ride, the next, his head had seemed to explode. If the cold water hadn't slapped him awake, he would be dead now. He'd come damned close, anyway. At best he could tread water, maybe dog paddle the length of a swimming pool. His childhood hadn't been the nice suburban kind that included Red Cross swim lessons. If it hadn't been for Megan Lovell, he wouldn't have had a chance.

He let his eyes close momentarily as he gave in to the hammering that should have split his skull. He would have liked to call the nurse for a shot of something, get rid of the pain. But that same shot would put him to sleep. And he had to think.

He had to decide what to do now. Was it conceivable that Saldivar had found him? But he couldn't have done so without help. When Mac tried to imagine any of the four or five people who might know where he was betraying him, he failed.

Which still left the indisputable fact that somebody had tried to kill him.

Who? Damn it, who? Had some other ugly part of his past caught up with him? Lord knew there were enough people out there with cause to hold a grudge against him. It was sheer bad luck if he'd stumbled across one of them, but sometimes it happened. Maybe he'd been a fool to go to ground in a place where he'd vacationed in the past, in a region where he'd once worked for the Bureau. Even though it had been years ago, it wasn't inconceivable that among the summer crowd of fishermen and boaters was one man who hated him.

Or, ludicrous though it might seem, he had to consider the possibility that in the last month he had happened on something he hadn't recognized, something that made him a threat. If so, they had made a big mistake trying to take him out. If a particularly nasty secret lurked behind the rural peace in these parts, he'd find it.

In the meantime, he would make damned sure Megan Lovell didn't suffer for her reckless generosity. He wouldn't be able to stop a high-powered rifle; but he doubted that one would be used. No, Megan would be far more likely to suffer a convenient accident, or be killed by a "burglar" she had panicked.

To be safe, he'd call his partner and have him make a few phone calls. If Saldivar's organization had found him, the odds were that the word would be out on the street. Saldivar would want to broadcast his success. He'd want to make it well known that the price for making a fool of him was high.

If Mac lived through another attempt on his life,

he might still have to run. But he had an obligation to the brave woman who'd pulled him out of the lake. And maybe more than that, Mac wanted to know for sure what he was running from. Curiosity always had been his weakness.

But when he finally closed his eyes and punched the call button, he wasn't thinking about the puzzle of who wanted him dead. Instead, he saw again Megan's hauntingly familiar face, with the blue eyes that looked clear to his soul.

"Hey, I hear you almost bit the big one."

Megan groaned, pausing on the sidewalk beside her Honda. "Don't listen to rumors."

Her big brother grinned as he tossed a duffel bag of what looked suspiciously like dirty laundry onto the roof of his low-slung sports car that he had parked just behind hers. "How can I help it? I think ten people called me."

"Starting with Mom, I'll bet."

"Dad, actually."

She groaned again. "What would I ever do without parents?"

John slammed the door of his Corvette and circled it. "Lose a few pounds?"

"Probably," she admitted ruefully. "I'm working today. After one of Mom's breakfasts, I'll just have to hope nobody tries to drown. I'd sink like a lead buoy."

The brother who had alternately tormented her and encouraged her through all of their childhood years now slung an arm across her shoulder while effortlessly hefting the duffel bag with his free hand. It still didn't seem natural that he had grown a good six inches taller than she. Nor that his cherubic, freckled looks had somehow become leaner, harder, so that now he was the kind of man who turned women's heads. Sometimes she caught herself watching him, looking for her gangly brother in the man he'd become. Maybe he had the same trouble with her. She had left home when she was fourteen to pursue her dream of Olympic Gold, training in southern California while living with the family of another swimmer. Then she had stayed away for college. Those missing years had left holes that could never be filled.

He waited for her to open the front door of the rambling old house in which they had both grown up before following her in.

"Don't you ever take a day off?"

She shrugged. "Somebody's sick."

"Yeah, probably went to a kegger last night." He raised his voice. "We're here!"

"Us and your dirty clothes," Megan murmured. "Why don't you grow up, big brother?"

He looked surprised. "What do you mean?"

"I can't believe you expect Mom to do your laundry! Or am I imagining the *eau de* dirty sock?"

"Uh . . ."

"Haven't you ever heard of the Laundromat?"

"I don't have time."

"Yeah, right." She punched him lightly on the upper arm. "Mom ought to dump 'em over your head."

"She doesn't mind."

"Sure. Hi, Mom."

Her mother, a slim, strong woman with dark hair and eyes as blue as Megan's, turned from the stove in the big, shabby country kitchen. "John." She frowned. "Megan, you're limping!"

Megan leaned over to kiss her mother on the cheek and inhale the aroma of cooking bacon and fresh-baked bread. "Just cut my foot on a rock. Don't fuss."

The minute the words were out of her mouth she felt a jolt. She'd said the same thing to him. Suddenly she saw him sitting in the hospital bed, his lean face tired, his brow furrowed. Had she been rude? So determined not to let him feel an obligation that she had been ungracious?

"Sit down," her mother said firmly. "John, put your laundry in the utility room and then set the table."

Megan and John docilely obeyed their mother's order.

"Who else is coming?" Megan asked.

"Linda's bringing the girls. Bill's off on a trip."

Megan's younger brother, Bill, drove long-haul trucks for a living, taking advantage of the stretches off to be as wild as ever. Megan had loved him the most of all her siblings, and had the least in common with him. Sometimes she wondered if she wasn't to blame for his wildness. If the whole family hadn't sacrificed too much to make her dreams come true.

But choices made couldn't be taken back, so she didn't think about the past again in the next two hours. Instead, she ate until her stomach whimpered, then cuddled her sister's six-month-old baby and got soundly trounced at the game of Memory by her six-year-old niece.

"Better watch it or I won't play with you again," she threatened, but the little girl with the dark curls only smiled impudently.

"You just don't pay enough attention."

"Beat Uncle John," Megan suggested. She grinned at her brother. "It'd be good for his character."

When she made her excuses a few minutes later, her father insisted on walking her out to the car. He was a tall, slow-moving man who liked to think before he acted. In his typical fashion, he was silent until they stopped on the cracked sidewalk.

"Megan, you'd be welcome to move home for a while."

She smiled. "Thanks, Dad. But I don't think there's anything to worry about."

The toothpick protruding from his mouth bobbed as he chewed slowly. There wasn't any special urgency in his voice. "The man you pulled out. What'd he say about it?"

"You mean you haven't heard on the grapevine?" she asked wryly. When her father didn't answer she sighed. "He claims not to know anything. He's been working for Jim Kellerman this summer. I guess he's a carpenter."

Mr. Lovell looked thoughtful. "I'll give Jim a call. Hear what he thinks about the fellow."

"Does it matter?"

He met her eyes squarely. "I don't like the idea of you mixed up in something dirty. Don't be too proud, Meg."

Something curled in her chest and she impulsively hugged him. "I won't be, Dad. I promise. But I really didn't see anything."

His expression was troubled. "Sometimes I think you're too independent."

She had been thinking the same, wondering how she would have reacted today if she hadn't learned too thoroughly how to be on her own. Would she have gone running home? Linda would have. Even

Bill all too often wanted to be bailed out of trouble. And John took his dirty laundry to Mom. It was an irony that she had come back to her hometown because she needed her family, but she couldn't let herself take too much from them.

Fortunately, business proved to be slow at the beach that day. In the late afternoon, dark clouds massed over the ridge and the mountains beyond. The lake still lay calm, but the air had an indefinable tension.

"I'll bet we're in for a thunderstorm," Megan said.

Rick, the oldest of the teenage lifeguards who worked for her, nodded. "Yeah. Shall we get everybody out?"

Megan studied the clouds. "Let people stay in the water for now. But keep an eye out. Don't wait for my order if you feel nervous."

Nods answered her. Megan turned to limp back to the boathouse. One large, noisy group of teenagers played volleyball on the grass court while a few families lingered at the picnic tables. The first crack of thunder and she'd send them all home, Megan thought.

Because there were so few people at the beach, she noticed him right away. One shoulder propped comfortably against the clapboard side of the boathouse, he was idly watching children shrieking on the merry-go-round. He wore faded jeans and an old green sweatshirt with the sleeves pushed up. He looked completely relaxed, unaware of Megan's approach, but she hadn't made a sound when he turned his head and their eyes met.

Wary, she stopped a few feet from him. "I thought you'd still be in the hospital."

"They gave me some pain pills and sent me home."

"I'm glad." She hesitated. "Is there something I can do for you?"

For a moment he didn't answer. Instead, his gaze moved down her body, and she was suddenly and embarrassingly conscious of how little she wore. The sleek, one-piece red Speedo racing suit bared far more than it covered. She knew that he could see her nipples tightening in an involuntary response to his casual, male assessment. That made her angry.

"Well?" she said sharply.

He was frowning when he looked back at her face. She had a feeling he was disconcerted by something; perhaps because of that, his voice was rough.

"I want you to accept my protection. Just for a few weeks."

"Protection?" It was her turn to be disconcerted. "You're not serious."

"I'm serious." She hadn't even noticed that he had a rolled newspaper under his arm, but now he held it out. "Take a look," he said brusquely.

Careful not to touch his hand, she accepted the newspaper, glancing down at the front page. It was the local weekly, the *Devil's Lake Caller*. Her gaze dropped below the banner to the grainy picture. Her own face, younger and happier, stared back at her. She recognized the photograph; it was one that had appeared in newspapers across the country. The reporter had pulled it out of the files. Beside it was a headline: Olympic Champion Saves Drowning Man.

Megan wasn't surprised that somebody at the hospital hadn't been able to resist passing the story on. In a small town, secrets were hard to keep. Looking back at him, she said, "So? It'll be a nine-day wonder. And they don't have *your* picture."

He made a choppy, impatient gesture. "Don't be a fool. The whole damn world is going to read about it. Megan Lovell pulled Ross McKenzie back from the dead."

"Hardly the whole world," she corrected. "Devil's Lake only has about a thousand permanent residents. That doesn't exactly qualify . . ."

"Surely you're not that naive." His tone was cutting, his lean face forbidding. "Every major newspaper in the country'll pick this one up. You were their darling. Now you're a heroine."

"Oh." She felt stupid. "I guess . . . But I still don't see . . ."

"Even if they left town, they'll read this."

"They" didn't need to be identified for her. She stared at him, a prickle of uneasiness sending an involuntary shiver down her spine. Bending her head, she read the article.

After a moment she looked challengingly back at him. "It says in plain letters that I didn't see the men clearly enough to identify them."

"And do you think they'll believe that?"

"Why shouldn't they?"

"Because their lives depend on it."

Again fear crept over her, made her voice low and husky. "Why are you really here?"

He was silent for a moment, and then his mouth twisted ruefully. "I told you. I owe you one."

She had been almost afraid of *him*, but when he looked at her like that, something deep in her stomach clenched in response. She used anger to cover it up. "And you want to pay me back by scaring the hell out of me?"

His gray eyes were bleak. "No. What I want is to keep you safe. Unless you're frightened, you won't take precautions."

Megan took a step back, shook her head. "This is ridiculous. If I need help, I'll call the police. I don't want a . . . bodyguard, or whatever you're offering to be. I just want everything to be normal."

"Normal?" Suddenly his tone was mocking. "What's normal for you, Miss Olympic Gold Medalist?"

"This," she said fiercely, gesturing at the beach. "Home. Friends. People I've known all my life."

He flicked the newspaper with one finger. "Not that?"

"Not anymore."

"I knew I'd seen you before," he said musingly. "I just couldn't figure out where. The minute I saw that headline, it fell into place. You were the one who looked so shy, who had a smile so sweet it melted America's heart. Wasn't that the line *Sports Illustrated* used? I remember watching a television interview of you one time, trying to figure out how a shy little girl had the guts to be a world-class swimmer. You might have been a kitten out of the water, but you had to be a shark in it."

"I'm not either anymore," she said starkly.

They stared at each other in dark silence, the emotional tension between them belying the fact that they were strangers. At last, as if compelled, he reached out and touched her cheek, slid his fingertips to her mouth. Her lips trembled before she jerked her head away.

"Go away," she said, in a voice that shook. "I'll accept your gratitude, but nothing else from you. Do you understand?"

"Oh, I understand." He looked frustrated. "Has anybody ever told you you're stubborn?"

She began to turn away, but glanced over her shoulder. "Frequently. I prefer to think of it as determined."

They both heard the low, distant growl of thunder. "Excuse me," Megan said calmly.

The water was still deceptively blue and peaceful, but the wall of stormclouds reared above the ridge and the air had become thick and damp-smelling. As she used the bullhorn to chase the last few swimmers out of the water, Megan heard another muted rumble from far away. After hanging the sign: No Lifeguard on Duty, Swim at Your Own Risk, she glanced back toward the boathouse. He was gone. So why wasn't she relieved?

An hour later the parking lot was empty, the lake turbulent. Lightning crackled above the ridge and thunder seemed to split the storm-dark sky. Megan waited alone under the eave of the boathouse. She was determined to stay until eight o'clock, when the beach officially closed. People could be dumb, and she didn't want to be responsible for a teenager driven by a dare.

Dusk was hastened by the storm. Within half an hour it was nearly dark. The sodium lamps shed an eerie yellow light that made her small car look even lonelier in the large, empty parking lot. Megan slowly became aware of her isolation. Each time lightning streaked the sky, she tensed, waiting for the crash of thunder. Feeling edgy, she tried to watch her car and the lake both, keeping her back to the clapboard wall of the boathouse.

Even if Ross McKenzie was right, she thought, if one of the wire services did pick up the story, it wouldn't have appeared yet. Probably even tomorrow would be too soon. But thanks to him, she was already listening for footsteps. Which was downright stupid. She had told him the truth. She wouldn't let herself be afraid of shadows. What she *would* do was call Pete Tevis when she got home and find out what he thought.

In fact, she might as well go home now. There wasn't even any traffic out on the road, far less anyone interested in a dip in the lake.

Megan grabbed her gym bag and headed across the grass toward her car. Suddenly headlights appeared out on the road, sweeping across the lot, mercilessly exposing her. Megan froze, operating on the instincts of a hunted small animal that knew movement would reveal it. When the car didn't hesitate, disappearing around a curve in a flicker of red taillights, she let out the breath that had been trapped in her throat and began to walk, faster and faster, until she was nearly running by the time she reached her car.

She looked warily in before unlocking the door, but the interior was empty. Once in the driver's seat, she locked the door again, absurdly reassured by the small precaution. A moment later, she turned the Civic out onto the road.

Almost immediately, headlights appeared in her rearview mirror. She studied them nervously. Had somebody been waiting for her? No, that was ridiculous. If some bogeyman was after her, he'd had his chance while she was all alone at the beach. He wouldn't follow her.

Nonetheless, she stepped harder on the accelerator. An instant later a second set of headlights appeared right behind the first. She couldn't figure out where either car had come from. She was glancing in the rearview mirror again when lightning flung a jagged bolt across the sky, nearly blinding her. Megan winced as thunder shook the world. She came to the stop sign at the highway and didn't even hesitate. Nor did the two cars behind her.

The other drivers had a perfect right to turn onto the highway also, she reassured herself. It was just coincidence that the two cars hovered the same distance behind hers.

When she turned again on the outskirts of town, the headlights were still behind her, but closer. In the next flash of lightning Megan tried to see the nearest car and failed. But her nervousness diminished as she passed lighted cottages, the small corner grocery. When she pulled into her driveway, both would no doubt pass by without even slowing down, the drivers never suspecting that they had frightened her.

Unless one of the cars wasn't that of a neighbor or wandering tourist. What had been a vague suspicion suddenly crystalized into angry certainty. He hadn't gone away at all. With or without her permission, he intended to "protect" her.

"Damn him," she muttered. As she turned too abruptly into the short lane that ended at her one-car garage, gravel spun under the wheels of her car. In her mirror she saw the first car seem to slow at the head of her driveway, then, illuminated by the lights of the second car, abruptly speed up. Throwing on the emergency brake, Megan flung open the door. Not at all to her surprise, the second car pulled in behind hers. As she stalked toward it, lightning flashed, then disappeared in a crash. But in the brilliant white light imprinted on her eyelids, she recognized him through the windshield.

Grabbing the handle of his door, she hauled it open. "Who the hell do you think you are, following me?" she stormed. "If I'd wanted you to know where I live, I'd have told you!"

His voice was as expressionless as his face. "I owe you, whether you like it or not."

"I will *not* be harassed!" she said. "Do you hear me? I'm going into the house and calling the police."

In the dim, filtered light from her porch she saw him frown. "Didn't you notice the company you had on the road?"

Megan felt another burst of fury. "I do have neighbors!" she snapped. "Amazing though it may seem, the lake road *isn't* private."

He said implacably, "That car was waiting for you. Do you know how easy it would have been to force you off the road into the lake? Nobody would ever guess it wasn't an accident on a night like this. I was beginning to think you were asking for it, staying at that damn beach all by yourself. Didn't you listen to a word I said?"

"I was doing my job," she retorted. "Anyway, I don't even know who you are! You're the last person I'm going to listen to."

Lightning shivered across the sky and the first splatter of rain hit her face. Megan braced herself for the thunder. In its aftermath she said, "And I meant what I said. I'm going into the house to call the police right now." With that she slammed his door.

She knew he sat in his car watching as she grabbed her gym bag from her Civic and headed for the ramshackle porch tucked behind lilacs and a huge, gnarled apple tree. She could feel the silence behind her as a tangible presence. Well, if he thought she was bluffing, he was going to be in for a big surprise, she thought angrily.

Seething, Megan had stomped onto the porch before she saw that her front door stood several inches ajar.

THREE

Megan froze, not even breathing. Light spilled through the crack onto the uneven boards of the porch, and she stared at the yellow streak as though it were a snake. At last, slowly, she eased back, crept down the stairs, without once taking her gaze from the door.

Where was Zachary? she thought suddenly, filled with new terror. She knew she'd left him out; she had worried that afternoon, when the storm began. The big retriever was petrified of thunder and firecrackers. But even if he'd been hiding beneath the porch, he would never have let someone break into her house.

When a hand closed lightly on her shoulder from behind, Megan gasped and whirled around. Ross McKenzie stood behind her. His eyes were intent on her face and she could feel his tension in the fingers that tightened on her shoulder.

"What's wrong?" he whispered.

Her mouth was trembling and she had to bite her lip to regain control. Her voice was a thin thread.

"My . . . my front door. It's open. I know I locked it."

She saw something hard and dangerous on his face as he looked beyond her. Releasing her, he reached beneath the denim jacket he wore over the sweatshirt. When his hand reappeared he held a gun. Megan barely stifled another gasp.

He gave her a look, jerked his head toward the cars. Megan didn't move. Leaving her with a last exasperated glance, he slipped through the shadows toward the porch. When lightning flared, he paused, but then he took advantage of the crash of thunder to climb the creaky stairs. He moved with the unnerving grace of a predator. Standing to one side of the door, he edged it silently open with the barrel of the gun, then vanished inside.

Megan hesitated, feeling the cold rain on her face, then reluctantly followed. It was *her* house, *her* dog who was missing. She had to *know*. And what if Mac shot Zachary? She had just steeled herself to poke her head around the doorframe when she heard him say harshly, "Freeze where you are!"

A muffled voice said, "What the hell . . . ?"

Shock clutched at Megan's throat. "Oh, no!" She was running when she reached the kitchen. The scene there horrified her.

Mac stood spread-legged in the doorway, gun held in both hands, pointed at the dark-haired man who had stopped halfway out of a kitchen chair.

"Mac, he's my brother! Don't shoot him!" She clutched at his arm.

Slowly he straightened, letting his hands drop so that the barrel pointed at the floor. His voice was dry. "I really didn't plan to, as long as he was smart enough not to go for a gun."

Bill sank back into the chair, swearing. "What in the hell is going on? Some maniac comes into your kitchen pointing a gun at me! Christ, he took ten years off my life!"

"I'm sorry," Megan said helplessly, sagging against the counter. "Bill, where's Zach?"

"Upstairs, hiding under a bed," her brother retorted. "I should have joined him!"

"I thought . . . Mom said you were off on a trip."

"I got in tonight," her younger brother said, his expression ironic. "I thought I'd say hello."

The man standing silently beside Megan slipped his gun into the shoulder holster hidden by his faded denim jacket. "You left the front door open a crack," he observed.

"The damn thing never latches. Is that a crime?"

"You scared Megan. She comes home at night, somebody's in her house. Don't you think she should be scared?"

"No," Bill said bluntly. "This isn't New York City. And, hey, I drop by all the time. Why would she think it was anyone else?"

Megan's emotions had been seesawing wildly, but now anger took precedence. "The only reason I was afraid was because *he* has been doing his damndest to scare me to death!" She glared at Mac. "You almost shot my brother, and all because you're hysterical over some invisible threat to me! This is the last straw! I want you out of my life!"

"Who the hell *is* he?" her younger brother asked, sounding a little plaintive this time.

There was a moment of silence. Megan's blue eyes locked defiantly with Ross McKenzie's narrowed gray ones. "You were glad enough to see me a minute ago," he said quietly.

"I was not!" she said, then added with supreme illogic, "If I was, it was only because of all your warnings!"

His mouth tightened. "What was I supposed to do, let you just wander in?"

"Yes!" He was too close to her, but she refused to back away. She didn't want him to see the small kernel of fear that was mixed with her anger. But there was more to it than that. She found it impossible not to be aware of him physically. He dominated the room with a dangerous charisma that she couldn't help responding to. She, too, wanted to know who he was, or maybe more accurately, *what* he was. He'd reached for the gun as naturally as she took a breath. He had a scar on his belly and killers on his trail.

She watched carefully for a reaction as she said flatly, "You're not a carpenter, are you?"

A muscle twitched beside his mouth. After a moment he looked away, staring at the rain-lashed window. Finally he sighed. "I can build a house. You might say I'm moonlighting at it."

"Why?"

"As a cover." He nodded toward the refrigerator. "Any chance you keep some beer in there?"

"That depends," she said stiffly.

The lift of his brow held sudden mockery. "Trying to bribe a police officer?"

Megan's mouth dropped open. Whatever she'd expected, this wasn't it. "You're a cop?"

"Actually . . ." he shrugged a little apologetically, "I'm FBI."

It was Bill who spoke up then, sounding hostile. "Can you prove it?"

Mac's gaze hadn't left Megan. Strangely, there

was something vulnerable in his eyes, as though he were waiting for some sign from her. Of approval? But why would he care what she thought of him?

Still watching her, he reached into the back pocket of his jeans and pulled out a leather case. Flipping it open, he held out a badge. Federal Bureau of Investigation.

Megan was lost. "But . . . I don't understand. Why are you *here*?"

Suddenly looking weary, he tossed the badge onto the worn kitchen table. "It's a long story. I'm going to have to trust you to keep it to yourselves."

Bill picked up the badge and stared at it in apparent disbelief. At last he shook his head. "Weird."

Mac glanced at him with wry humor, then back at Megan. "Do you mind if I sit down?"

"What? Oh! Of course. I'm sorry. You probably still have a headache, don't you?"

He lowered himself carefully into one of the pressed-back oak kitchen chairs and stretched out his long, muscular legs, wincing in obvious pain. "Yeah, you might say so. I suppose I'd better take one of the damn pills."

Megan hurried to get him a glass of water while he produced a small bottle of white capsules from the pocket of his jacket. "Haven't you been taking them?" she asked.

"Didn't feel too bad earlier." He popped one onto his tongue and took a long drink of water. Then he gave her a lopsided smile. "How about that beer?"

"You shouldn't mix . . ." Megan began automatically.

He interrupted gently, "One won't hurt. And I'll bet your brother could use one, too. Shock is tough on the system."

Megan opened her mouth to argue, then sighed. "All right! But you have to talk in payment. I want to know what's going on. Does Pete Tevis know who you are? And those men. Who were *they*?"

"Pete Tevis?" Bill echoed. "I don't get it. This whole thing is crazy!"

Mac said, "I'll explain as much as I know. But what I tell you can't leave this room. Do you understand? It isn't just my safety at stake."

Bill glanced swiftly at Megan, then back at Mac. "Yeah, sure, I understand. I guess."

"I think you missed the first installment," Megan told him as she got the beers. "Somebody bopped him over the head the other day and tossed him into the lake. Unfortunately for their plans, I pulled him out."

Her brother absorbed that in silence. "Did you see them?"

"Yeah, she saw 'em all right," Mac said drily.

"But not well enough to identify," Megan interjected.

Mac took a swallow of beer, coolly holding her gaze. "They're not going to believe that."

She sat down and propped her elbows on the table. "And *I* still think you're being paranoid."

He grimaced. "Yeah, well, it's an occupational hazard, I'll concede that. In this case, I just don't want to take a chance." He shrugged out of his denim jacket, leaving it draped on the back of the chair, and took another swallow of beer.

"But what's *this* case?" Bill asked in bewilderment. "I mean, crime is not a big problem at Devil's Lake. We have an occasional boat stolen or maybe somebody has a little too much to drink and slugs somebody else. Not exactly your thing."

Megan scarcely heard her brother. It seemed so strange, the three of them sitting casually around her kitchen table talking. Mac didn't fit here. The leather holster crisscrossing his broad shoulders only accentuated his air of toughness, the guarded look in his gray eyes. In contrast, her handsome, blue-eyed, dark-haired brother seemed very young. Even Mac's voice had a rough edge to it, and she had the feeling he never spoke without carefully weighing his words first.

Now he shrugged. "I was hiding here. And you're right. I picked it because I used to come fishing here and I remembered it as being peaceful. Not the kind of place I'd meet former . . . ah, acquaintances."

There was a moment's silence. "You know," Bill said. "I don't think I heard your name."

Megan waited curiously for his response. She couldn't help remembering his hesitation when she had asked for his name that morning in the hospital. Was it only yesterday? He'd said it as though the syllables sat awkwardly on his tongue. Without consciously realizing it, she had found it hard to think of him by a name. It had been easy enough to picture him, tall and lean and dangerous.

He didn't look at Bill as he said quietly to Megan, "I lied to you. My name's not Ross McKenzie. I'm sorry. I was uncomfortable doing it, when you'd just saved my life."

"I knew you were lying," she admitted.

"Yeah?" He smiled ruefully. "I must be losing my touch."

She just waited.

"My friends call me Mac. That much is the truth. I was born James McClain."

"Born?" That seemed a strange way to put it.

"I've used a few other names along the way." He said it with outward indifference, but Megan thought she heard bitterness he couldn't quite hide.

Obeying a sudden impulse, she touched his hand. "Okay. Mac it is."

His eyes searched hers for a long moment, and then he smiled. The smile was charming, sensuous and very dangerous. Megan's pulse gave a ragged jump.

"So why the fake name?" she asked.

He raked his fingers through his hair. "My last assignment was undercover. I spent almost a year penetrating a particularly nasty crime family in Miami. Mostly into drug distribution. Anyway, my cover got blown by somebody I'd busted before. Sheer bad luck. We had enough to indict some of the lower echelon, but not the kingpin. And since Saldivar doesn't take kindly to what he regards as betrayal, he put out a contract on me. It seemed like a good idea for me to disappear for a while. We'll get Saldivar sooner or later. We're close. In the meantime . . ." He shrugged.

"Is that how you got the scar?" Megan asked softly.

Mac nodded. Bill looked from one face to the other, but didn't ask any questions.

"So . . . how did they find you?"

"I don't think they *did* find me. Although I'm checking out that possibility, too."

She frowned. "But why would anyone else want to . . ."

"I've made enemies."

"In Devil's Lake?"

He rubbed his forehead, and again Megan noticed how tired he was. There were shadows under his eyes and his face looked drawn. "Not to the best of my knowledge," he said. "Like I said, I picked the place because I came fishing here years ago. I had good memories. And, hell, it seemed like the back of beyond! But I did work here in the Northwest. Maybe somebody who hates my guts has taken up fishing, too. It's always possible."

"You haven't recognized anyone?" she asked tentatively.

"Not a damn soul."

"But, then, isn't it likelier that—"

"How?" he interrupted. "How the hell would they have found me here?"

Megan tried to think, but she knew so little about the alien world he lived in. "Somebody must know where you are."

"A handful of people." He suddenly frowned. "This part isn't your problem."

"But I'm involved!"

"I want you as uninvolved as possible," he said harshly. "When I can be sure nobody is interested in you, I'll disappear again."

Megan tried to imagine what assuming another identity would be like. A strange town, a strange name, anonymity of the soul as well as the body. Wouldn't you begin to wonder yourself who you really were? She found the thought strangely disturbing.

"You make it sound so easy," she said.

He looked surprised. "It *is* easy. There's nothing to it."

"But your family, your friends." Why was she arguing? Why did it seem to matter so much? "Don't you have a cat or dog? And a home? And . . . and things?"

Even Bill was staring at her now, puzzled by her sharpness. Mac's expression was quizzical.

"Things can be replaced," he pointed out. "You are who you are no matter who or what's around."

"No." She shook her head forcefully. "I don't believe that. We're *shaped* by the people we love. 'No man is an island . . .' "

"I've heard that." His voice was hard. "I don't believe it. If it were true, I wouldn't exist at all."

Again she was caught by his bitterness. "What do you mean?"

"Nothing." The chair legs scraped as he abruptly pushed it away from the table. After pitching the beer can into the trash under the sink, he stood looking out the window, his back to them. He rubbed his neck with one hand, as though trying to release tension, but his voice was almost expressionless. "I work undercover a lot. Do you know what would happen if you spent all your time pining for some damn dog? Or your own TV? Sure you forget who you are. That's the only way you can function. You have to *be* the slimeball you're pretending to be. But then you walk away from it, from who you were, and that person doesn't exist anymore." He turned to face her. "Nothing to it."

Something painfully close to pity stirred in her chest. "I see," she said carefully. Why did she want to touch him, to smooth away the harsh lines on his face?

"So?" he said. "Are you going to be smart enough to drop out of sight?"

"It's not for me."

"Damn it!" He slapped his hand on the counter. "Don't be a fool!"

Megan didn't say anything, just stared stubbornly back.

He looked at Bill. "Can't you convince her?"

Bill had the bewildered expression of a spectator at a football game who'd been asked to take the quarterback's place. "Convince her? To do what? I don't understand."

"She needs to take a vacation away from here for a while. Just until this whole mess is cleared up."

"But if she didn't see anything . . ."

He swore. "I didn't know it was possible to be so naive!"

"Better naive than paranoid," Megan said sharply.

His laugh was short and humorless. "Let me spend the night at least."

She reacted with instinctive alarm. "What do you mean?"

"Obviously not what you're thinking. I'll sleep on the couch, keep out of your way."

"That might not be a bad idea," Bill said. "Unless . . . Hey, why don't you come home with me? You can even have my bed. Or sleep in the truck. They'd never find you there."

"They, they, they!" Suddenly angry, she jumped to her feet. This whole thing was ridiculous—no, insane! She refused to be frightened out of her own house! But she couldn't help remembering those headlights that had appeared from nowhere in her rearview mirror, the car hesitating at the head of her driveway. "Enough already! If it'll make you happy, you can sleep on the couch, I don't care! But don't think for a minute that I believe any of this!"

"Hey, calm down," Bill said. "He's just trying to take care of you."

She gave her brother a fierce look. "Drop it! I

agreed, didn't I?'' When neither man said anything, she stalked out. Using some of her adrenaline, Megan snatched sheets and blankets out of a closet and wrenched the couch in the living room out with a clatter. With quick, angry movements she made it, trying not to think about Mac's long, hard body sprawled carelessly on those pristine sheets.

When she looked up, Mac stood in the doorway watching her with an odd expression. "I'm sorry," he said in that rough-edged voice. "You're having to pay a price for saving my life. That's not fair."

Somehow her anger had slipped away. Megan gave the pillow a last punch and straightened. "We always pay a price for our choices."

"It's the price others have to pay for us that hurts."

She knew that too well. Trying to change the subject, she said at random, "You don't even have a toothbrush."

"I'll survive."

"You could go get your . . ."

One dark brow quirked. "Things?"

"Yes, things!" she said acerbically. "Surely even you like to brush your teeth and put clean underwear on in the morning?"

At that he grinned, and again Megan was startled by the transformation. Laughter warmed his face, made him wickedly charming. Her heart seemed to lurch, and she bit her lip. He wasn't for her; she had to quit responding as though he were. He was a man who'd known so many names he had probably forgotten some of them, a loner. Soon he would be gone, without looking back. If she let him touch her heart, even a little, she would be sorry.

"Okay. If your brother will hang around until I

get back, I'll go get my 'things.' " With that he vanished from the doorway.

A moment later Bill appeared. "He's gone," he said abruptly. "Megan, I don't know if we should trust him. His story's so far out, it's like something on TV! And he's made damn sure we can't call anybody to check on him. I don't know. Maybe you should come home with me instead."

It was hard for Megan to separate into small compartments the muddled feelings she had for Mac. Fear and uncertainty and anger and a deep, unreasoning attraction that she suspected had had something to do with her capitulation. But trust?

"I'm pretty sure he's telling the truth," she said slowly. "I saved his life and he doesn't like the idea of owing anybody. Unnecessary or not, this is his way of paying off the debt. I think I should let him."

Bill continued to hover in the doorway. He looked uncertain. "Listen," he said awkwardly. "Is there something . . . well, between you two? I sort of felt in the way. I mean . . ."

"No!" She tried to moderate her voice. "No. Really. There's nothing. It's just . . . different, when you've been through something together like that. We're strangers but we're not. It makes us uneasy with each other. That's all."

From her brother's expression, Megan didn't think she'd convinced him. She hadn't even convinced herself. There was an odd thread of tension between her and the man who'd come so dramatically into her life. It was more complicated than mere physical attraction, although her feminine instincts told her that it was mutual. But she didn't understand it and wasn't sure she wanted to.

Refusing to let herself get too analytical, Megan

forced a smile for Bill's benefit. "I could use a cup
of tea. How about you?"

"Did you already have dinner?"

"I took a break at work."

Her brother shrugged. "I'll have another beer."

Twenty minutes later Mac returned with a small
suitcase. Bill left immediately, after telling Megan in
an undertone to call if she wanted him.

Megan closed and locked the front door. She was
proud of her casual tone when she said good night
to Mac. "I'm tired. It's been a long day."

They were in the narrow hallway. But when she
took a step forward, Mac didn't move, and she hesitated. If he didn't stand politely aside, she would
have to brush by him to get to the stairs. It seemed
safer to wait.

"You don't have to run away from me," he said.
His voice was quiet, his body relaxed. Yet she had
the sense of him coiled and ready, the stillness an
illusion.

"I'm not running away," she lied. "I think you
should get some rest, too. I'll bet the doctor didn't
intend for you to chase after me all day."

Amusement showed in his gray eyes. "Is that what
I've been doing?"

"When you weren't scaring me to death," she
said tartly.

"I meant well."

"If I didn't believe that, you wouldn't be here."

"You're just humoring me, aren't you?"

"That's right," Megan agreed. "Now if you'll
excuse me?"

Mac smiled and stood aside. But as she passed,
Megan made the mistake of pausing. Her glance met
his and she saw the way he looked at her, the smile

gone but his mouth curiously tender. Her feet seemed rooted to the floor. Slowly, almost reluctantly, he took a step toward her and his hands gripped her upper arms. She could feel his warmth and her heart climbed into her throat. Her voice didn't sound like her own. "I don't think . . ."

"I'm sure you're right," he said huskily. His eyes held an odd light and he let go of one of her arms to lightly grasp her chin instead. She couldn't have moved to save her life. All the tumult of the last days seemed to have been leading to this, as though it were all that mattered.

"I should let you go," he murmured. But now his thumb traced soft patterns on her cheek.

"I . . . I . . ." Where were the words? But it was too late, she knew, when she saw his gaze lower to her mouth. The next moment he was kissing her.

Gently, oh so gently. His lips brushed hers, touched her cheek as lightly as a snowflake that melted against her warmth. She made a small, shaky sound, flattening her hands on his chest. He groaned and for just an instant his mouth hardened with demand and his arms tightened. Heat shuddered through Megan, frightening her with its insistence, and she resisted, pushing blindly against his chest. Immediately he released her and stepped back, his hands falling to his sides.

Breathing hard, they stared at each other in taut silence. What was she doing? Megan thought in horror. He was an almost total stranger who would be gone soon, the man he'd been here forgotten. Nothing to it, he'd said. But she couldn't forget so easily.

His eyes were hooded, his voice rough when he said, "I'm sorry."

Megan only nodded jerkily. Without a word she passed him and went up the stairs to her bedroom. He still stood unmoving in the hall below when she gently closed her bedroom door.

FOUR

Kissing Megan Lovell was one of the stupidest damn things he'd ever done. Mac turned restlessly on the thin, hard mattress, no nearer sleep than he had been an hour ago. What the hell had he been thinking?

He didn't like even acknowledging his attraction to her. He owed her. He couldn't afford to complicate that. Without much success, he tried to convince himself that his uneasiness was rooted in his dislike of owing that kind of debt. He was used to operating without ties. His partner, well, that was different. They had a working relationship. Neither had ever tried to becomes buddies.

Mac's every instinct screamed for him to run, but he couldn't desert Megan, no matter how stubbornly she dug in her heels. And who knew? Maybe he was wrong. Maybe the two hit men had congratulated each other on a job well done and never looked back. Maybe no stringer for UPI would notice the article in the *Devil's Lake Caller*. Maybe he and Megan would get lucky.

Unfortunately, Mac didn't believe in luck.

He did finally sleep, but not deeply. The throaty bark of a dog didn't quite fit in Mac's dream, and he surfaced so quickly, he was alert before his eyes were open.

The barking came from upstairs, though even as he sat up and reached for his gun he heard the scrabble of claws on the stairs as the big golden retriever bounded down, baying all the way. Mac swung his legs off the bed and rose soundlessly. The dog hit the bottom of the stairs and slid on the wood floor as he turned toward the kitchen. If there had been an intruder at all, he was probably long gone.

Then Mac heard the tinkle of glass breaking. Zachary's barks deepened to a roar. Mac slipped across the hall into the dark kitchen right behind the dog. The big windows at the dining end allowed just enough light so that he could see a silhouette. The bastard was climbing through the broken window even though eighty pounds of fierce muscle and teeth was launching itself at him.

A flurry of movement, and something rammed into the dog, who fell with a howl of mixed pain and anger. Mac covered the kitchen at a run, crouching to make himself as small a target as possible.

"Freeze!" he snapped, locking into a stance and taking aim.

Things happened too fast then. He couldn't tell whether the dark shape in the shattered window hesitated at all before Zachary scrambled to his feet and lunged again, knocking a kitchen chair against Mac's bare legs.

He stumbled sideways. The intruder swung something that slammed against Mac's shoulder, driving him to his knees. Mac flung the chair away, but by the time he was up, the intruder was gone. Still barking, Zachary leaped through the window and disappeared in pursuit.

Mac swore and headed for the front door. He dove out it into the shrubs, than ran across the damp grass to the protection of a tree. At the end of the driveway the retriever's barks were cut off at the same instant a car engine started. Mac abandoned caution and sprinted down the driveway. The gravel cut into his bare feet.

Tires squealed. The car was gone by the time he reached the road.

Mac swore again, bitterly. If it weren't for the damn dog . . . Yeah, if it weren't for the dog he might not have awakened at all.

Where *was* the dog? Mac whistled. Silence. He'd better get some shoes on, and a flashlight. Limping, he returned to the house. The front door still stood open, but now light poured onto the porch. He shook his head in disbelief. Why didn't she just have invitations engraved?

Inside, Megan waited, her heart pounding, her mother's walking stick clutched in sweaty hands. It had been all she could do to make herself creep down the stairs. The silence was now more terrifying than the crashes and Zachary's ferocious barking earlier, when she had been pulled out of a deep sleep.

When, with a lurch of relief she recognized the man who appeared in the doorway, she slowly lowered the stick.

He glowered at her. "Why don't you open the back door while you're at it?"

"Don't yell at me!" she retorted. "You're the one who left the door open."

"Yeah, and what if I hadn't been the one who walked through it?" He kicked it shut.

She hoped her voice didn't sound shaky. "I figured I was safe. Not too many burglars work with bare feet."

Not that she *felt* safe. There was nothing about the angry man in front of her to reassure the timid. Especially not if the timid happened to be a woman. He'd been dangerous enough lying in a hospital bed. Stalking toward her, the next thing to naked, he made her heart rise into her throat. He wore black sweatpants that hung low on his hips and emphasized how narrow they were in contrast to wide shoulders and sleekly muscled chest. His legs were long and powerful, the gun that he carried in one hand a violent match for the scar that slashed across his stomach. Megan was forcibly reminded of the last time she had faced him, right here in this hall.

Swallowing, she took a step back. "Where . . . where's Zachary?"

"I don't know. Do you have a flashlight?"

She retreated a few more steps. "I . . . I'll get one."

He strode past her into the living room, where he snatched up a sweatshirt. Megan closed her eyes. She wouldn't watch him get dressed. She wouldn't.

Zachary, she reminded herself. Think about Zachary. Her cowardly, afraid-of-thunder dog who had sounded far from afraid. Please, she prayed, please don't let him be dead. If he was, it would be her fault, because she hadn't listened to Mac.

"You can open your eyes now," Mac said drily.

Flushing, she did. A black sweatshirt matched the pants, and he had shoved his feet into shoes. "The

. . . the flashlight,'' she faltered. ''I'm sorry. I'm not used to things like this.''

They both heard the scratch on the door at the same moment. Mac lifted the gun and jerked his head at her to open the door. With trepidation she obeyed.

''Zachary?'' The big golden retriever hobbled through the opening. Megan fell to her knees and hugged the soft animal. ''Oh, sweetie, are you all right?'' A comforting wet tongue slopped across her face.

Mac locked the door and laid the gun down on the hall table. ''Let me take a look.''

She sank back on her heels, keeping a reassuring hand on the dog's broad head. Mac eased a hand over the retriever's legs, and finally shrugged. ''He's not in too serious shape.''

''Are *you* all right?'' Megan asked, guiltily wondering about the crashes.

Mac started to shrug, then grimaced. ''Yeah. More or less. Let's take a look at your kitchen.''

Megan followed him, trying to keep an anxious eye on both man and dog. Zachary limped and Mac moved stiffly, but—as he'd put it—neither seemed to be in very serious shape.

Mac snapped the light on, and Megan stood in silence beside him. The large window looking out toward the lake had been shattered. Shards of glass glittered on the floor and gaped wickedly from the window frame. The table had been shoved to one side and one chair lay in the middle of the kitchen floor. Beside it was a four-foot length of two-by-four.

Suddenly cold, Megan crossed her arms, hugging herself. ''Did he . . . did he get inside?''

She felt Mac's gaze, but didn't meet it. ''He had

a leg swung over the windowsill when I got in here. He wasn't about to let a dog stop him."

A shiver traveled up her spine. She looked at the two-by-four, grayed by weather. It could have been picked up off the top of anybody's pile of scrap lumber. Would it hold fingerprints? she wondered. Would this stranger who'd taken over her life *let* her call the police and find out?

"You know what that means," Mac said.

"No. No, I don't."

"It means he wasn't some local kid trying to steal your TV. The dog would have scared him off."

Megan shivered convulsively. "You're scaring *me*."

"Good." His blunt tone was brutal. "I hope to God you'll listen to me now."

Anger snapped her out of her paralysis. "I wish I'd never . . ." Megan stopped abruptly.

"Never seen me?" He looked at her sardonically. "Just don't expect me to agree with you."

She closed her eyes. "I didn't mean that. You know I don't. I just . . . I just wish none of this was happening."

"Megan . . ." His large hand cupped the side of her face and lifted it so that she opened her eyes. The gentleness in those dark gray eyes scared her more than the sound of shattering glass had. "I'm sorry," he said roughly. "I wish you hadn't been involved, too. If I could change it, I would. But I can't let you pay a price for saving me."

Holding herself very still under his touch, she said, "I'm not a child . . ."

"I've noticed."

He didn't have to say anything more to make her

acutely conscious of the awareness in his eyes, the twist of his hard mouth.

"Don't do this," she whispered.

"Do you think I want to?"

"I don't know!" The words came out too loud, and she jerked away. "I don't know *you*!"

He swung away. "Go to bed," he growled. "We'll talk about it in the morning."

"Shouldn't we call the police?"

"Tomorrow. Go on."

Something in the rigidity of his back and the sandpaper quality to his voice silenced any argument she might have made. She had no reason to trust him, but she had told her brother the truth: up to a point, she did. And he was right; the kitchen wouldn't look any different tomorrow. But she would feel differently in daylight, safer.

And so she went, without another word, ignoring the part of her that wanted very badly to find out what would happen if she stayed.

Mac didn't let himself watch her go. That would have been a luxury he couldn't afford. He already knew he wouldn't sleep the rest of the night. There was no guarantee that their visitor wouldn't come back once he calmed down and realized he'd faced one man and a dog, not a phalanx of local cops.

Not that he'd have slept anyway. Last night's kiss had been even stupider than he realized. He supposed he'd thought one taste of her would satisfy his curiosity. Instead it had awakened a hunger he hadn't felt in a long time. Hunger for soft curves and a tender touch, for passion and dark nights and a throaty voice calling his name. No, worse yet. What he'd suddenly remembered was the forever he had dreamed about as a child. Then he had imagined a mother who would kiss him good night, who would bake fresh cookies and take him to Little League baseball, be a helper in his first-grade classroom and drive on field trips. Well, that wasn't exactly what he had in mind now. He laughed without any amusement at all. No, right now forever had something to do with unfathomable eyes and sweaty nights, cold water and arms that would never let go.

He'd take the sweaty nights. None of the rest were for him. He hated water, cold or otherwise. And he had learned to prize the freedom that was the one legacy of his childhood. A woman like Megan Lovell could endanger it.

That didn't mean he could put her out of his mind. In any other circumstances, he would have tried to seduce her. One kiss had tantalized him, but if he could have all of her, he'd be satisfied. One long night . . . Yeah, one long night that he wouldn't have. He owed her. That meant protecting and serving, not using her to satisfy sexual needs.

It'd be a hell of a lot easier if only her blue eyes didn't sometimes become smoky with awareness just as sexual as his own. He wished he didn't know how her mouth softened under his, how pliant her graceful, athletic body became. He wished he didn't know that she was the kind of woman who would never let go once she made up her mind to love a man.

Megan woke to the smell of bacon and coffee. She showered and dressed in blue jeans and a white cotton sweater, then used the excuse of braiding her hair to dawdle.

But the moment couldn't be put off. She went quietly down the narrow stairs, but was unsurprised when, without even turning his head, Mac said, "Do you drink your coffee black?" He stood in front of the stove, spatula in hand.

"No, I like the works." She accepted the proffered mug and made a production of stirring in sugar and powdered cream, looking over the kitchen. The shattered glass had been swept up and a piece of plywood covered the broken window. She could almost—but not quite—forget last night. "How's Zachary?"

Mac took some eggs out of the fridge. "Limping. Maybe he should see the vet."

Irrelevantly, she asked, "Where did you find the bacon?"

"I jogged down to that little store."

"Zachary'd like the grease on his breakfast."

Mac flashed her a rueful grin that weakened her defenses. "I couldn't find his breakfast. He's annoyed at me."

The big retriever flopped his tail from where he lay with his chin resting on his empty bowl.

Her own mouth curved into a smile. "He does look hopeful. Believe it or not, his food's in the hall closet. I buy it in such big bags, that's the only place it would fit."

Prying the bowl from under Zachary's chin, she filled it and Mac poured hot grease over the brown nuggets. When Megan plopped it back on the floor in front of the dog, he dove right in.

Behind her, Mac asked, "Scrambled or over easy?"

"Have you ever heard of cholesterol?"

When she turned around, the smile was gone from his mouth. "Lately I haven't worried too much about turning sixty. The day I relax, I'll cut down on cholesterol.''

Her gaze lowered involuntarily to the front of his black sweatshirt where it covered that long red scar. She knew his head must still ache, too. How could she argue?

''Scrambled,'' she said.

They talked about total trivialities during breakfast. What vet she took Zachary to. Who to call to replace the windowpane. Where she normally grocery-shopped.

Megan wasn't really hungry, but she ate anyway. She didn't let herself meet Mac's gaze until she pushed her empty plate away.

Then she said flatly, ''Are you going to call the police?''

''I don't know.'' For the first time Megan noticed the signs of weariness on his face. The grooves in his cheeks were carved more deeply, and the fan of lines beside his eyes showed his age in a way they hadn't before. ''That depends on you.''

''I'll move home with my parents,'' she said. ''They've already offered me my old bedroom.'' ·

She didn't like the idea, but she knew after last night that she wouldn't feel safe alone. And what was the alternative? Letting Mac stay to protect her? He scared her more than the phantom enemy did. He was still a stranger and always would be, because his outlook was so different from hers. How could she, who so valued home and a town where she knew everyone, be attracted to a man who could walk away anytime? She couldn't decide whether he was so sure of himself, he didn't need others to define him or whether he was soulless, a stranger even to himself. But the answer didn't matter. The problem did. She was desperately attracted to a man without roots, one who would not understand her need for her own.

But he was shaking his head. "That's not good enough. Damn it, Megan. Look how fast they hunted you down. They must have discovered they'd failed almost immediately."

"The newspaper article . . ."

"Can't have hit the big papers yet. Face it. They must have hung around, waited just to be sure. They're professionals. Either that . . ." he leaned forward as if to emphasize his point, "or else they're locals. People who already knew you. Either way," he shook his head, "failing once won't stop them."

In agitation Megan set down her coffee cup. "It's you they want, not me. Maybe they knew you were here last night. Did you ever think of that?"

"Of course I thought of that!" he snapped. "But I called my partner this morning and he tells me word on the street is that Saldivar is still looking for me. He's mad as hell. There should be some hint that he found me. I can't believe it's him. And that leaves an open field."

"I'll be safe with my parents," Megan said stubbornly. "I promise I'll be careful not to be by myself. You can forget about me. Just . . . just do whatever you have to."

Maddeningly, he shook his head again. "Somebody who would murder you in cold blood isn't going to stop at adding other victims. You'd be endangering them. Do you want to take that kind of chance?"

Megan stood up abruptly and pushed her chair aside. "This is crazy! Why am I listening to you?"

"Because somebody broke into your house last

night. You're smart enough not to buy that kind of coincidence."

Her fingers closed painfully on the back of the chair. "We have burglars just like anyplace else, you know. Maybe the police could find fingerprints or something if you'd let me call them. Or are you afraid they'll punch holes in your story?" she challenged.

Really smart, Megan, she thought. If the guy's a pathological liar, did she want to back him into a corner?

His eyes narrowed and a muscle spasmed in his jaw, but no other reaction showed. "All right," he said at last. "If that's what it'll take to make you take this seriously, we'll call them."

"Good," she said boldly. "Do you want me to do it?"

His tone was dry. "Why not? You probably know everyone on the force."

She dialed quickly, her back to Mac but conscious of his gaze on her. She asked for Pete Tevis. When he came on the line, Megan told him about the attempted break-in.

He didn't waste any time on sympathy. "I'll be right over."

Mac stood up. "Do you mind if I take a quick shower?"

"No, of course not. There's shampoo and everything. Help yourself."

To keep herself busy, Megan cleared the table and washed the dishes. All the while she pictured the man upstairs in *her* shower. Naked, water sluicing down his lean body. His wet hair darker, plastered to his head. When the shower stopped, she imagined him stepping out, scrubbing his hair with the towel, wrapping it around his waist. Drops of water beaded on his tanned skin, muscles rippling as he moved.

"Don't be an idiot," Megan said aloud, hooking the damp dish towel over the refrigerator-door handle. As her father had commented once about a boy she had a crush on, "He puts his pants on one leg at a time." At the time she had daringly retorted, "Yeah, but once they're on he looks better in them than anybody else does." Mac did, too. What other man was sexy in a pair of sacky sweats?

Mac timed it perfectly, coming down the stairs just as Pete Tevis knocked on Megan's front door. At the sight of Mac, something tightened in her stomach. Damn it, it just wasn't fair! No one man should have cheekbones like that and shoulders wide enough to shelter a woman and cool gray eyes that could see right through her. She had a lump in her throat when she opened the door.

Pete's gaze immediately went past her to the man who'd obviously just showered and was coming from the cottage's only bedroom. It hadn't occurred to Megan how that might look.

"Megan," The deputy sheriff nodded. "Mr. McKenzie."

Oh, boy. She'd forgotten the name thing. Would Mac expect her to lie for him? How much did he intend to tell Pete?

His expression was impassive, but he pulled his badge out of his back pocket and flipped it open. "Actually, it's McClain. James McClain."

"You don't say." Pete Tevis took the badge, sounding no more surprised than Megan had been when she found out Ross McKenzie wasn't really his name. Wouldn't you think the man could lie better than that? she thought.

"I'm going to have to ask you to keep what I tell you to yourself."

"Well, now." Pete handed back the badge after a careful scrutiny. "I can't promise that. Not until I know what you have to say."

The two men's gazes clashed for a long moment before Mac nodded reluctantly. "I'd do the same."

They studied the kitchen, then went outside to look for footprints and tire prints and whatever else policemen expected to see. At last they ended up sitting at the kitchen table, Megan listening as Mac told his story to the graying deputy.

Only when he got to her part in it did she contribute. "This guy used an old piece of two-by-four to break the window. Of course that set Zachary off. Surely some hit man would cut the glass or jimmy the lock or *something*."

"She's got a point," Pete said.

"Come on," Mac said impatiently. "They *want* it to look like a burglary that went wrong."

Pete shook his head. "Could be. But I've got to tell you, we've had a rash of burglaries at beachfront places. Six or seven in the last month. This could be no more than another one."

"How did they get in?"

"Pretty much the same. Broke a window. Only difference is, nobody was at home when the other places were picked clean."

"This guy had to know someone was here," Mac said. "There was a car out front, a big dog in here carrying on. This SOB broke the window *after* Zachary started barking, not before. Damn it, no burglar would do that."

Pete nodded at Megan. "Mind if I have a refill of that coffee?" When she took his cup he admitted,

"That's pretty unusual. Kids, though, they get drugged up, they're not always smart. You must've scared the hell out of him."

"I'm not so sure," Mac said thoughtfully. "That was the interesting part. A kid should have been yelling at me not to shoot. This guy clobbered me with the two-by-four and took off. Car started so fast, I think he had somebody waiting for him, too. If I could have seen the license . . ."

"Yeah, we'd have had something to work on," Pete agreed. "As it is, I'll send one of the boys out to dust for fingerprints, just in case. I'm betting we don't find any."

Mac nodded. Pete continued. "Now, as to your problem, I'll tell you what. I'll keep what you told me to myself, so long as this business doesn't go any further. If Megan's attacked, or you are again, that promise is off."

Mac nodded. "I can't ask any more than that. Now will you try to talk this stubborn woman into doing something smart? If she would just go visit some friends for a while . . ."

Megan didn't give Pete a chance. "I will not run away. So don't waste your breath. I'll move home with my parents for a week or so, but that's my best offer."

Mac's mouth hardened. "Damn it, Megan . . ."

"No." She gestured passionately. "Even Pete's not sure this wasn't a garden-variety burglar! You're making some big assumptions. I just can't accept them. I mean, the whole thing is nuts! I'm committed at the beach for the summer. What are they supposed to do if I don't show up? School starts for me in less than four weeks. I need to start preparing my room—"

"Four weeks might be long enough," Mac interrupted.

"No." She stared mulishly at him.

He glowered back. "Tevis, help me out here."

"It might not be a bad idea," Pete said. "A little vacation couldn't hurt."

"No."

Mac growled something under his breath and turned his intensity toward Pete. "Can you give us some practical help? Keep an eye on Megan?"

The deputy let out a long breath and shook his head at the same time. "I've been thinking about it, but I don't see how I can. We can drive by the beach a little more often, maybe by here, too, but I just don't see how I can come up with anything else. We're stretched too thin. Do you know how big this county is, how many miles of roads there are? As it is, our response time is embarrassing. I try to explain this story to the boss, it's going to sound like the bogeyman to him."

Megan could see that Mac hadn't expected any other answer. His frustration was obvious in the grim look he gave her.

"Then you're stuck with me day and night," he said. "Don't even try to argue."

She wanted desperately to do just that. How could she bear to share her small house with him for days, weeks, a month? Was she being stubborn for no good reason?

But she just couldn't believe somebody was out to hurt her. In the dark, knowing her house had been violated, she had been scared. Now, in the sanity of daylight, the whole thing just didn't make sense. *She hadn't seen those men.* They knew how far from shore they had been when they dropped Mac into the cold depths. They had chosen the spot for good reasons. If they hadn't been able to see her, they would know damn well that she couldn't have identified them. Mac was paranoid. Maybe it was an occupational hazard, but it wasn't one she shared.

No, if anybody here was hunted, it wasn't her. Couldn't he see that he was putting her in danger by staying?

Only, she hadn't quite forgotten last night. What if she had heard the window shattering, her dog suddenly silenced? Footsteps crossing the kitchen. On the stairs. What if Mac hadn't been here? A shiver raised goosebumps on her arms and she slowly nodded.

"Okay. Just don't . . ." Don't what? Touch her? Kiss her? Look at her with eyes that had darkened to charcoal and a mouth so sensuous her own trembled?

None of those were the things that really scared her. She knew she could trust Mac to protect her physical well-being. It was her emotions, her heart, her innermost self that were in jeopardy. Unfortunately, he was the one who threatened them.

". . . just don't make me trip over you," she finished, her voice almost steady.

Somehow she didn't think she fooled either man.

FIVE

Mac knew damn well that Megan resented him. He was a reminder of things she'd rather forget, a ghost she'd raised herself. One impulsive, gutsy moment, a decision she couldn't take back, and look what a prize she had hauled out of the water. He was closer to a shadow than a flesh-and-blood man. The thought left a bad taste in his mouth. He did his best to make sure no one else noticed him, but that didn't do Megan much good. She knew he was there, wherever she went.

In his long and varied career he had learned how to blend in, though his face and his height sometimes made it hard. At the beach nobody paid any attention to him. Bring a towel, a book, wear a gray sweatshirt and jeans on cold days, athletic shorts and a Miami U. T-shirt on warm ones, and just hang around. Far as he could tell, there wasn't anything better to do in Devil's Lake anyway. People who weren't out waterskiing were at the beach or barbecuing in their own back yards or maybe hanging a fishing line from one of the docks.

After a couple of days of trailing her everywhere without incident, Mac finally made the decision to leave her alone at the beach on busy days. He'd be sleeping on her couch for the rest of his life if he didn't take some steps to find out who'd conked him on the head and why. If she was ever safe, it was in the midst of a few hundred screaming kids.

The first thing he did was stop by Jim Kellerman's construction office, where he had worked these last months. When he walked in, Kellerman was digging through a dented file cabinet stuffed to overflowing. The balding man glanced over his shoulder and grunted.

"Back from the dead, I see."

"Yeah, I had a little accident," Mac said.

"So I hear. Pete Tevis gave me a call."

Mac had arrived at a decision on the way over. Kellerman was an older man, taciturn but fair. Megan had mentioned that her father had known him for years and considered him a friend. Mac was chafing already at the restrictions his situation placed on him: no access to data bases and police files, no authority to question people or dig into their affairs. If somebody local was responsible for his problems, his best attack was to investigate the people he'd encountered through his construction work. Kellerman wasn't going to let him sit and read files, note names and phone numbers, who paid and who didn't if he thought Mac was a drifter who'd done a decent job for two months, then not bothered to show up for work one morning. Sometimes you had to take chances; Mac had decided to take one with his ex-boss.

"I need some help," he said. "Do you have a minute when we won't be interrupted?"

Kellerman looked him over in silence, his blue eyes shrewd. "Now's as good as any other time," he finally agreed, lowering himself into his squeaky office chair behind the battered gray desk. Mac sat, too, then pulled out his badge and a wallet full of genuine ID he'd recovered from a safety deposit box. He'd lost the fake ones; maybe they tossed that wallet in the lake with him. He didn't know.

The older man barely glanced at the badge and ID. "You implying something's wrong with my business?"

Mac shook his head. "Nothing like that. I'm the one with problems, not you."

And so he explained, for the third time in the last few days. He was growing to like the people here in Devil's Lake. Each time he'd expected interruptions, questions, hysteria. Instead, Kellerman listened as thoughtfully as the deputy sheriff had. His only reaction was to pop a peppermint candy in his mouth and suck on it.

"You were mighty lucky Megan was around to fish you out of the lake," he said at last.

"I understand you know her father."

He grunted again. "I've known Megan since she was a toddler. Unusual kid."

"Not your usual lifeguard," Mac commented. He'd be interested to hear what the home folks thought of her.

Kellerman shook his head. "She's got to be rolling in bucks. Her face was everywhere after the Olympics. She still does some endorsements. I understand she's agreed to be a color commentator at the next Olympic games, too. But, you know, you'd never guess any of it. She's the girl next door. My granddaughter was in her kindergarten class last year, loved her. This stuff at the beach . . ." He shrugged. "She must enjoy it."

Enjoyed yelling through a bullhorn at kids who didn't seem to have the sense God gave them? Mac thought incredulously. Well, why else would she do it?

He grimaced. "The main thing I've discovered about her is that she's stubborn as hell."

"You don't get to be the best in the world at anything if you're not," the balding man pointed out.

Mac rubbed a hand over his face. "I suppose so. And God knows I have good reason to be grateful she's stubborn."

Kellerman nodded. "So what do you want from me?"

Mac told him.

Kellerman frowned and swiveled his chair to gaze in silence out the window toward the huge metal building that garaged the construction equipment. "How many jobs did you work on?" he asked.

"I've been trying to think. Maybe twenty, counting some one-day jobs."

"You know, those fellows who knocked you on the head asked specifically for you. Molly remembers that much. They called instead of coming in."

"Lucky for her."

"Yeah, so Pete said." The older man shook his head. "Things like this don't happen in Devil's Lake."

Mac didn't say anything.

Kellerman turned in his chair to face Mac. "Pete tell you the address they gave is an empty lot?" Mac had checked it himself two days ago, but he only nodded. His ex-boss looked him directly in the eye. "You can have the run of this place as far as I'm concerned. If you can't find something, ask Molly. I'll tell her to give you a hand. I can give you some time once you have a list of people you want to know more about. Half our customers I've known for years. There aren't too many strangers in Devil's Lake.''

Mac offered Kellerman one of his rare smiles as he stood. ''Thanks.''

The balding man rose, too. When he came around the desk, he clapped Mac on the back. ''You were a hell of a worker. You want to give up that FBI stuff, you know where to come for a job.''

Mac's laugh was rueful. ''You never know. I might be ready for something a little more restful one of these days.''

He'd known it wouldn't be easy, but the next few days were among the most frustrating of his life. Devil's Lake was a small community; there *had* to be some bad apples. Mac just couldn't find them. Yeah, Edith Whitney was a classic old maid who liked vicious gossip; her curtains twitched whenever anyone went by her small frame house. Chuck Lowe beat his wife; everybody knew it. The school board was starting to have their suspicions that a high school English teacher hired the year before was sleeping with a student.

But that was it. Mac couldn't find a damn thing on anybody he'd worked for. Or anybody else, for that matter. He retraced the steps he'd taken that summer, stopped by houses where he'd remodeled and chatted with their owners. Between Megan and Jim Kellerman, he'd heard more about the residents of Devil's Lake than he really wanted to know. That, and he watched for strangers—or for that one face that wouldn't be strange to him.

He found strangers, all right, but they tended to be families renting summer cottages, or dedicated fishermen who were out on the lake at the crack of dawn and then back out again before dusk. Hell, none of them would have been willing to miss the prime hour for fishing just to attack him. They would have aimed for noon or midnight instead.

Anyway, what were the odds of him having encountered an old enemy? He had worked in the Pacific Northwest, but years ago. Back then he had been younger, thinner, his hair regulation length, his clothes dark-gray suits instead of jeans and sweats. Somebody might have recognized him this summer, but it would have taken the devil's own luck. The thought brought an ironic smile to his hard mouth.

Over and over, he came back to the part that stuck in his craw. How likely was it that two enemies hunted him at the same time?

The days of deceptive calm weren't helping his cause with Megan, either, he thought in frustration. They were driving home from the beach, Mac behind the wheel. Megan was frowning as she stared ahead through the windshield, somehow removed from him. She was becoming more restive in his presence, more confident by the day that the bogeyman was his fantasy. She'd be ready to kick him out any day, he knew.

Only, he wasn't going anywhere.

Mac didn't trust the quiet any more than he did most people. Having come up empty-handed locally, he was becoming reluctantly convinced that Saldivar had indeed found him. If so, his old enemy was keeping it very quiet. But then, Saldivar wouldn't like admitting to failure. This time he'd want to see Mac's body before he'd crow triumph.

But how had he been found? Mac squeezed his fingers so tightly on the steering wheel that they hurt. *Damn it, how*? He had traced enough people on the run to know how to disappear himself. He hadn't made any of the usual mistakes: he'd never used real ID or credit and bank cards, he hadn't taken up the same kind of work here or joined a favorite national organization under his new name. If he'd made a mistake at all, it had been going to ground in a place he had been before. But how in God's name would Saldivar know where Mac had gone fishing once ten years before?

For what good it did, once they were home he called his partner, Norm Eaton, for the tenth time. Megan had disappeared into the kitchen, making noises about dinner.

When he answered, Norm sounded as edgy as Mac was beginning to feel.

"Damn it, McClain, you're a sitting duck! You've got to do something, and you know what I vote for. Run again. Make Saldivar start all over. We'll get him sooner or later, you can count on it. Buy us some time."

"I can't leave the woman," Mac said tersely. "I owe her."

"Make her run, too."

Mac gave a snort of near amusement. "I wish I could."

"The only other choice I can see is to set a trap. With you as bait, the bastard won't be able to resist it."

Mac reached up to knead taut muscles on the back of his neck. Across the small living room and through the arched doorway he could just see a corner of the kitchen. Every couple of minutes Megan passed through his field of vision as she stepped between sink and stove. He liked the way she moved, quick and graceful, her stride more contained than the hip-swaying walk of most women.

"That's what I wanted to do in the first place," he said wearily. "Now I can't. Short of arresting her and tossing her in the local jail, how do I keep her from looking like bait, too?"

Silence was his answer, and he was left with the same problem. He had to find a way to remove Megan Lovell from this whole mess. As each day passed, he became more determined. She had risked her life for him. He had to pay her back in kind. Then he could move on with his life. He could forget her.

Megan brooded as she worked on dinner. She tore the lettuce into shreds and chopped carrots with quick hands, hardly conscious of what she was doing.

He was there all the time, at the edges of her consciousness. Megan wanted to forget him and pretend life was normal, that this summer was just like every other one since she had come home again. But how could she, in a house as tiny as hers, in a town so small his constant presence at her side must be causing talk?

What he succeeded in doing was awakening her fear every time she saw him. Her rational side was convinced the threat was illusory. On a more primitive, emotional level, however, she couldn't help being afraid. Sometimes she thought it was Mac himself who frightened her.

She would glance over her shoulder at the beach

and there he was. Nobody else seemed to notice him, and she couldn't understand why. He was extraordinarily handsome with the bones of a male model and that dark blond hair curling on his neck. But what struck her most was the quality of danger he possessed. He was a dark presence, an unsmiling, watchful man who never quite fit in with those around him.

Megan slowly realized, though, that she was more nervous when he *wasn't* there. It was then that she suffered doubts, wondered about that smiling father who approached her, the two vaguely Hispanic men who strolled past with fishing poles and tackle boxes. It was then that she felt vulnerable, and grateful when Mac reappeared.

She hated her dependence on him. This was her hometown, the one constant in a life of change, of new coaches and different swimming pools that all looked alike, of teammates who sometimes envied her and friends who didn't understand her drive to be the best. Devil's Lake was where she felt safest, most herself; where she belonged. Now she was being robbed of that sense of security. In saving a life, she had changed her own, she thought bitterly.

She could hear Mac's voice in the other room, but didn't try to make out words. It sometimes seemed to her he was playing games. Cops and Robbers. Or maybe she just *wanted* to think it was a game.

Puffing out an impatient breath, she grabbed a hot pad and pulled the biscuits out of the oven. "Dinner's ready," she called.

He raised his voice. "Be there in a minute."

She rolled her eyes. How cozy. They sounded like a couple who'd been married for ten years. Megan slammed the cookie sheet down on the counter with complete disregard for the sea-green Italian tiles she had tediously installed. With a pancake turner she flipped the biscuits off the sheet, her movements jerky, tension bound up in her muscles until she felt like a steam engine with the escape valve blocked. Explosive.

A biscuit landed on the floor and she felt like kicking it. *Damn it*. Before she could vent her childish anger, Zachary disposed of the biscuit in one gulp and Megan sighed, dumping the rest into a basket.

When she heard footsteps approaching she made herself close her eyes and take a couple of deep breaths. Why was she letting this ridiculous situation get to her like this?

Stupid question. She knew the answer, even if it was about as clear as a stew, with as many ingredients. She felt manipulated. Scared. Couldn't help wondering if she was being foolish. Stubborn. All the things he called her.

And then there was the kicker.

She turned to face him, and felt the same response: the leap of her heart, the lurch in her stomach, the warmth deep in her core. The remembrance of his mouth on hers, the gentleness and heat.

And she wanted him to kiss her again, despite everything. Fortunately, pride and some remnant of sense ensured that she do whatever it took to hide that.

"Would you grab the salad out of the fridge?" she asked in a voice so calm she amazed herself.

"Dinner smells good," he said, obligingly opening her refrigerator.

"It's a casserole my mom always made." Which Megan bothered to cook once in a blue moon—if then. With just herself to think about, she tended to settle for instant dinners: soup and crackers, a salad, something from the freezer department at the grocery store. She didn't even have to ask herself why she had suddenly turned into Little Miss Homemaker.

Setting the hot chicken dish on the table, she said, "Speaking of my mother, she called earlier. Wants us to come to dinner tomorrow."

She was gratified to see alarm on his face. He set his fork down. "You're kidding."

"Nope," Megan assured him, with a certain amount of malicious pleasure. "She wants to meet you."

Mac looked as if he would have liked to groan. Instead he said reluctantly, "I guess she has the right."

"I told her we'd be there." Megan coolly took a bite.

He raised an eyebrow. "What if I had said no?"

Megan smiled. "I'd be delighted to go alone."

"Like hell." His mouth twitched. "Point made."

"Good," she said provocatively. "Just think what a social calendar I could make up, and here I have a guaranteed escort."

"Until you get blown away for being stupid," he agreed.

"By you?"

"I'm tempted to do something almost as drastic," he muttered.

"Oh?" God, had she batted her eyelashes at him?

His dark gray gaze raked her face. "Take three guesses."

Belated self-preservation and an accelerating pulse was enough to make her back pedal. "I'd just as soon not. I know I rank low on your list of favorite people right now."

His eyes met hers, shocking her with the blatant sexual hunger she saw in them. "I wouldn't say that." His expression became hooded and he returned his attention to his dinner. "I'm doing my damndest to keep you alive, aren't I?"

"Mac . . ." She hesitated. "Are we going to go on like this forever?"

"I'd rather not," he said impassively.

Megan felt a stab of something she was dismayed to recognize as hurt. What, did she want him to pretend this wasn't a duty? Sure, he *liked* sleeping on the too-thin mattress of her sofa. He *liked* following her around like Zachary on a leash. He had nothing better to do, no ambitions for the rest of his life.

More cynically, she thought, he's probably tired of this identity. Time to become somebody else.

She lifted her chin in a challenge he couldn't mistake and said, "Then what are you doing about it?"

He met her gaze warily. "You know what I'm doing about it."

"Those two men didn't come from Devil's Lake, did they." It wasn't really a question.

He carefully buttered a biscuit. "I never thought they were year-round residents. Joe Carlson at the marina would have recognized them. That doesn't mean they weren't weekenders, or even summer renters. Or hired hands for somebody who *does* live here."

"People in this town aren't like that."

He snorted. "For God's sake, Megan, you know better than that."

"No, I don't," she said stubbornly.

He pushed his chair back from the table in a sudden burst of frustration she recognized as a match for hers. "All right, damn it! They don't live here. What the hell difference does that make?"

Her stomach was in knots and her hands were curled into fists underneath the table. "This is your problem. You brought it here. You have to get us out of this."

His eyes narrowed. "I could do a hell of a lot better job if you weren't complicating it. Right now, I'm a bodyguard. You're tying my hands."

Now she pushed back from the table and stood up, suddenly angry. "Who is complicating whose life? This is *my* home! My car, my job, my town! You want me to go sit in a hotel room somewhere staring at the walls for weeks or months, so you don't have to worry about whether I might catch some fallout from *your* problems. Well, guess what? I have no intention of doing that!"

"No kidding." Mac's mouth had a sardonic twist. "Somehow I figured that out."

"Good." Megan shoved the chair in and began gathering dishes, clattering them together. "Are you done eating?" she snapped.

"I have to admit I've kind of lost my appetite."

"If you want dessert, there's ice cream in the freezer." *What a perfect little hostess*, she thought, exasperated.

"Megan." He rose from his seat with an effortless grace that always tweaked some sexual cord in her makeup. Before she had a chance to argue, Mac took the pile of dishes out of her hands. His jaw was set, but his face was expressionless. "I'll clean the kitchen. You've been waiting on me hand and foot. It's my turn to do some of the dirty work. Why don't you go take a bath. Read a book. Call a friend. Just don't pay attention if you hear things breaking."

When she didn't move, he smiled, though it didn't quite reach his eyes. "Don't you have any sense of humor? I won't break anything."

Did he think she'd melt at one little smile? Knowing she sounded grumpy, still she said, "I used to have a sense of humor."

He set the dishes on the counter and turned to face her. "Yeah, well, it's hard to find anything funny in somebody trying to kill you, I will admit."

"Or in somebody trying to save you from nothing," she said, with no softening in her voice.

His eyes narrowed. "Well, let me tell you something. Right this second, I'm trying to save you from me, so I suggest you take my advice and get the hell out of this kitchen." Just like that, tension was pulled so tight between them one wrong word would snap it.

Megan's outrage was mixed with something that scared her a little. Did she *want* to push him a little too far? But this was *her* house, *her* kitchen. She couldn't let him order her around like this, all in the name of being chivalrous. "I'll go when I'm good and ready," she said childishly.

"Fine." Mac's voice was as gravelly as the bottom of Devil's Lake. He strode by her and grabbed dishes from the table, then slapped them on the counter. She heard a crack and started forward.

"You said you wouldn't break . . ."

He swore under his breath. "God, you make it hard to keep my temper."

"So lose it!" she snapped, forgetting the dish. "Just once I'd like to see *you* act like a real human being."

Without once looking away from her, he picked up a glass from the counter and flung it against the wall. It shattered and fell in glittering shards on the floor. Openmouthed, Megan stared at him.

"You think I'm not frustrated as hell?" he asked. "You think it's easy following you around like a goddamned dog every day? How do you think I like tossing and turning every night, knowing you're right upstairs?"

Her voice sounded a little squeaky when she said, "What's that have to do with anything?"

His gray eyes burned hers. "Everything," he said. "And you know it."

"No." Was this why she had pushed? she wondered wildly. So that he would tell her how badly he wanted her? Was her ego so starved? "I'm . . . not exactly irresistible," she whispered.

He made a despairing sound in the back of his throat and then pulled her into his arms. She recognized, just before his mouth claimed hers, that *this* was what she had wanted, not the words.

And then he was kissing her with intent, white-hot desire that seared her. She couldn't think, or even respond, only leaned against him and accepted his savage need. His teeth hurt her lips, but the pain sent heat shooting through her veins. Somehow her arms had wound themselves around his neck and she was so close to him that the weight of his arousal pressed against her stomach. Megan whimpered and her head fell back.

The next instant, he pushed her away. She wobbled, and he said hoarsely, "Unless you want to clean up this kitchen by yourself, you'd better get out of here."

"But . . ."

Except in his eyes, which glittered, she could see

no trace of the lover. His expression was grim, his face hard. "Now," he said implacably.

Without a word, she turned and fled. Just as she reached the doorway, his rough voice stopped her. "I *will* get out of your life one of these days."

She nodded, hiding the sting in her eyes, and left him in the kitchen. Safely in her bedroom, Megan sagged into a rocker. Dear Lord. After everything that had come before, he had meant to reassure her with his words. Why, oh, why couldn't she find some comfort in the thought of his departure? she wondered desperately.

Was it because she didn't believe he ever *would* leave?

Or because she didn't really want him out of her life?

Megan had told her parents about Mac the day after the attempted break-in. She'd made the announcement with some trepidation. Mac was the target of cold-blooded killers, not exactly an ideal roommate from a parent's point of view.

Actually, it had been her mother she had spoken to on the telephone. Megan's announcement that a strange man was now living with her—strictly for her safety, of course—was followed by a moment of silence during which Megan winced.

Then her mother said, on what was clearly a rush of relief, "Oh, thank goodness! We've been so worried."

Of course, Megan thought on the way to her parents' house that next evening, they hadn't met him yet. She had a feeling their relief at having her guarded day and night might dissolve once they saw what Mac looked like. Presumably they prized her safety above her virtue, but what mother in her right mind wanted a killer whale in the bay with her minnow?

Mac had let her drive, which always made her nervously conscious of her impulsive style. One of the world's great drivers she was not. Mac never talked much when they were on the road, and his silence usually quelled her own chatter. She guessed he didn't want to be distracted from his watchfulness. She would see his gaze flick from the side-mounted rearview mirror to the road ahead and then back, never pausing for long. Maybe his presence should have made her feel secure, but it had the opposite effect. All she could think about was what he expected to happen. A car bomb? A rifle shot through the windshield? A fiery crash?

Worse yet, since last night they had scarcely exchanged a word. What was there to say? Yet the silence had become thick, charged with a quality as dangerous as any car bomb.

"Thank God," she muttered, once she'd parked the Civic in her parents' driveway.

Mac raised a brow.

"Nothing," Megan said. "Come on."

"Wait here for a minute."

She rolled her eyes but obliged. He climbed out of the car, his hand just inside the faded jean jacket that looked so casual but presumably hid a shoulder holster. His restless gaze scanned the block while she waited. At last he nodded. "Okay."

"Thank you," she said sweetly, her sarcasm provoking a twitch of that hard, sexy mouth.

"Never say I don't do anything for you," he commented, surprising her.

Some demon drove her to respond in kind. "Would

I say that? After all, you washed the dishes last night.''

"Your priorities never cease to amaze me."

"Ditto," she retorted, then opened the front door and raised her voice. "Hi, Mom, Dad."

"Oh, Megan." With suspicious alacrity, her mother appeared in the kitchen doorway. "How nice. You must be Mr. McClain."

"Mac," he said, holding out a hand. "Nice to meet you."

Megan's mother smiled and took his hand. "I'm Anne. And my husband . . ." She glanced over her shoulder. "Oh, there you are, dear. Mac, this is Megan's dad, George."

"George." Another handshake as the two men appraised each other. Megan waited with a certain amount of apprehension for the result. Not that she would be able to tell what Mac was thinking, or her dad, for that matter.

Eventually they moved on into the big country kitchen, where Mrs. Lovell was working on dinner. "Chicken with artichoke hearts," she announced. "One of Megan's favorites," she told Mac. "She does so little cooking on her own, I worry about her. Those TV dinners don't have enough nutritional value to keep a mouse alive! She'd never eat a decent home-cooked meal if she didn't come here."

Mac's amused gaze met Megan's, and she cursed herself for blushing. *Thank you, Mom*, she thought.

"Actually," Mac said judiciously, "she might surprise you. She's been feeding me decently."

Obviously startled, her mother turned to look at her. "Really?"

Megan mumbled, "Well, it never seems worth the

effort when it's just me. But Mac has an appetite like a horse. I have to feed him, don't I?"

"You could starve me out," he suggested.

"What an idea!" Mrs. Lovell sounded shocked. "I'm sure Megan appreciates what you're doing for her."

Megan crossed her arms. "No, I don't! This whole thing is ridiculous. Why do I have to keep saying that? This is Devil's Lake, for crying out loud! You all sound like you think we live in New York or something! I mean, when's the last time we had a murder here?"

"If it weren't for you," her father put in quietly, "we'd have had one last week."

"Yes, but—"

"No *but*," her mother interrupted. "If someone wanted to kill Mac once, there's no reason to think they won't try again."

"Which is all the more reason for him to go away," Megan said defiantly. She wasn't altogether sure who she was arguing with. Was it her parents, Mac—or herself? And what was the point? She had resigned herself to Mac's presence. Hadn't she?

She was dismayed to see her father—her calm, even phlegmatic father—shake his head. "You saw them, Meg. If they were willing to kill once, why not twice? Only makes sense, from their side of the whole thing."

Defeated, Megan said, "Okay, okay. I'm just being hysterical. Ignore me. Hey, Mac does, anyway."

"I wouldn't say that." In a moment of stillness weighted by unacknowledged emotions, Mac and Megan looked at each other.

Megan tore her gaze away, only to catch an odd

expression on her father's face as he watched Mac. Sadness?

"Megan," Mrs. Lovell said briskly, "why don't you set the table. George, do you suppose Mac would like a glass of wine or a beer?"

"I wouldn't mind a beer," Mac agreed, smiling at Mrs. Lovell. With resignation Megan observed her mother's blush. On the receiving end of that devastating, sexy, yet somehow sweet smile, what woman wouldn't blush?

By tacit agreement, the whole subject of Mac's reason for staying in Devil's Lake was dropped over dinner. They ate on the back porch, coolly shadowed in the early evening, with a magnificent view over the lake. Megan was unpleasantly reminded of the night she had stopped beside the road after work; of the purple shadows and shimmering glow, the stark backdrop of mountains and the gathering quiet. So impulsive, so unimportant that decision had been—and how frightening the consequences.

The conversation rambled from national politics to fishing. "I don't hunt," Mac said. "I see too many ugly examples of what guns can do. Shooting one is cold necessity, not fun."

"I'm not a hunter myself," Megan's father agreed. "Most of the folks around here are. I just don't like killing anything that doesn't have scales."

"You don't even like killing the things that do," her mother teased. "Half the time you make me knock them on the head."

"Have to admit," Mac said laconically, "I throw 'em back most of the time."

Megan groaned inwardly. Soul mates. Wouldn't you know? Her peaceful, amiable, slow-talking father and the man sitting across the table from her who had cold eyes and the instinct to run toward danger, not away. On the other hand, her dad had fought in the Korean War, which she had never been able to picture. Maybe that was where he had learned to hate killing. Maybe the two men had more in common than was immediately obvious.

"Where are Linda and John tonight?" Megan asked.

Her mother sipped from a mug of herb tea. The dinner plates had been replaced with peach pie and tea. She said vaguely, "Oh, up to their usual, I suppose. I didn't want to overwhelm Mac, so I didn't invite either of them."

"And I suppose Bill's off again."

Her mother only nodded.

"I've met Bill," Mac said.

"So we heard," Mr. Lovell agreed. "Scared the pants off him."

"Yeah, well, he scared the pants off Megan." Mac sounded unapologetic.

Megan opened her mouth to argue, then shut it. What was the point in opening that discussion again?

"We'd better be getting home," she said instead. "I want to stop by the school tomorrow for a few minutes before work. They've changed my room, I'm down in the old wing now, so I'd like to take a peek. I might not have as much bulletin-board space."

Her mother gave a quick look at Mac, who had frowned. Tentatively she said, "Do you really think you'll be able to teach in September?"

Megan straightened. "Why wouldn't I?"

"Well, if this is still unresolved . . ."

"If nobody has taken a pot shot at me by then, I

think we can forget the whole thing, don't you?" She stood up. "Mac, are you ready?"

He set down his half-empty cup of coffee. "Sure. Always ready to serve. That's me."

Megan's mother chuckled and Megan rolled her eyes. Damn it, was she always bad-tempered, or did Mac just bring it out in her? " 'Night, Dad." On sudden impulse, she bent to kiss her father on the cheek, though she was normally undemonstrative. " 'Night, Mom," she said, turning.

Apparently moved by the same impulse, her mother gave her a quick hug and whispered, "Be careful."

Megan carried the words and the feel of her mother's embrace home with her. Her father's cheek had felt softer than it used to, she thought a little sadly; she had noticed new lines on it tonight.

Had they all shared the same chill that had made her want to reach blindly for her mommy and daddy? Had they all wondered, just for that fleeting second, whether they would see each other again?

Ridiculous, she told herself for the second time that evening, stealing a glance at the shadowed face of the man who sat watchfully beside her in the small car. If somebody wanted to kill her, he would have tried again, not let days pass. Mac's profession encouraged paranoia, hers hope. She would not let herself be infected.

SIX

It began to rain the next afternoon, a soft drizzle that steadily hardened. By five o'clock the downpour left the beach empty. Megan and the lifeguards had retreated to the boathouse. She stood in the open doorway and watched the driving rain turn the lake to a battered sheet of iron. She listened to the drumming and smelled the damp.

Where had Mac gone? she wondered. Had he even been here near the end?

On the sunny days, with the beach crowded, she was impatient with his presence. Now, conscious of the nearly deserted parking lot, she began to feel uneasy.

"Well," she said, "I suppose we might as well hang it up."

"You mean, we get a night off?" one of the guards exclaimed with mock incredulity. "Wow, we can have a beach party."

Megan smiled. "Right. Just not here."

They separated to finish bringing the equipment in and hang the No Lifeguard on Duty sign. She overheard two of the boys talking about a kegger and some girl with big boobs. Great. What did she have to look forward to? A cup of hot chocolate? Carefully *not* thinking about Mac, she stuck out her tongue at the boy's back, the immature gesture curing her of a momentary worry that she might have gray hairs to go with her less than well-endowed chest.

Megan took care to be ready to leave at the same time as her lifeguards. The parking lot was as gray as the lake. Like the others, she ran to her car, but she was still drenched when she got there. Just as she reached it, the driver's-side door swung open, offering refuge.

"Come on, get in," Mac said. His deep voice should have startled her but didn't.

She bumped her elbow on the steering wheel before she managed to squeeze herself and her duffel bag in and slam the door. She gave a shiver and shook drops off her hair. "Lovely weather."

"Look at it this way," Mac suggested. He had the seat pushed back to give him leg room and looked enviably dry and comfortable. "You get to go home and take a hot shower, have dinner, read a good book . . ."

"Are you trying to send me to bed at eight o'clock again?" Megan asked tartly. "What if I feel like partying?"

"Do you?"

She made a face. "What do you think?"

"I think we should buy a pizza on our way home. Maybe a six-pack."

"Now you're trying to get me drunk."

That mouth quirked into an irresistible grin that deepened the crease in one cheek. "Now *you're* being difficult."

Conscious of a reckless stirring inside, Megan retorted, "Comes naturally."

"I've noticed," he said, lazy humor in those gray eyes that were so often as chilly as the rain outside the car. "So, what do you say?"

"Pizza it is," she agreed, and started the car.

Half an hour later, they sat at her table sharing a hot pizza loaded with everything but the kitchen sink. She had toweled her hair, combed it out, and left it loose to dry. When she had changed clothes, Megan ignored the sweats that would have been cozy and instead chose a pair of black leggings and an oversize cotton sweater.

Mac's first comment was, "You look about sixteen years old."

"Sweet sixteen," she said flippantly, reaching into the refrigerator for a can of beer.

"But I know you've been kissed."

Did he have any idea how his voice gave away his thoughts? Megan wondered. It had just become a little grittier, the texture as tempting as the hard line of his mouth.

"Can't I pretend?" she said lightly, and opened the pizza box. "Help yourself."

Abruptly he asked, "Why do you take a summer job? You don't need the money, do you?"

Megan gave her standard answer. "I get bored. What would I do all summer? Sit around with my feet up?"

"Travel. Do some more endorsements." He smiled. "Read some good books and go to bed early every night."

She looked away from that too perceptive gaze. "I traveled when I was a swimmer. It was fun then, but I saw every place. China, Australia, Mexico

City, you name it, I've been there. Now I just want to be home again."

"Trying to recapture your childhood?"

She concentrated on separating another piece of pizza from its mates, winding a string of cheese around her finger. "Maybe," she admitted, then startled herself by sharing a realization she had only recently made. "When I'm doing something useful, I feel like I belong here. When I'm not, I don't."

Mac set his beer can down and studied her. What did she know about not belonging? he thought with bitterness he seldom acknowledged.

She looked so young in some ways, until you saw her eyes. Vivid blue, they should have been smiling, but they weren't. Her expression was too often guarded. Like his own.

"That's not how people around here think of you," he said carefully. "You're theirs. They're proud of you."

She shrugged with resignation. "That's just it. I'm different."

"You must have wanted to make people proud of you. You didn't swim only for yourself, did you?"

Again those extraordinarily blue eyes met his and he saw layers of complex emotions. "No. How could I? Do you have any idea how many people you owe, by the time you make the Olympic team? My family sacrificed for me, the town sacrificed so I could afford to train in California, the country was counting on me . . . I'd get these piles of letters from people who were trying to be supportive, telling me how proud they were that I was an American, and do you know how you end up feeling?" When he silently shook his head, she finished in a burst. "Burdened. Carrying everybody else's expectations, not just your own. How could I lose? I'd have disappointed so many people. And, do you know, even though I won, I still feel guilty. Especially with my brothers and sister. Too much of my parents' time and energy was spent driving me to practice, getting me to meets, eventually paying for me to live away so I could train with other swimmers at my own level.''

He didn't dare move. If he had tried to comfort her, take her hand in his, argue, she would close up, he knew. So he said dispassionately, ''Why do you feel guilty? Do your brothers or your sister resent you?''

Megan let out a long breath. ''No. Of course not.'' She smiled ruefully, shattering the mood. ''That doesn't mean I can't torture myself, does it?''

''Nah,'' he said. ''It's one of life's little pleasures.''

She chuckled, a delicious ripple that sounded so carefree, he congratulated himself. But then she gestured with the can of beer she'd been working on for twenty minutes. So much for getting her drunk.

''You know everything about me. Now it's your turn. C'mon, give.''

He automatically evaded the question. ''Hey, you already know me. We're opposites. I don't care about places.''

''Or *things*,'' she said. ''I remember. What I don't know is, why.''

Mac took a swallow of beer and said, ''I grew up in foster homes. That doesn't exactly give you roots.''

She bit her lip. ''And here I've been whining about not belonging,'' she said softly. ''I'm sorry.''

''It's hard being different, no matter why you are.''

Her blue eyes searched his face. "You said foster *homes*. Did you move a lot?"

A familiar feeling of shame made him look away from her. "Ten or twelve times. I wasn't exactly . . . cooperative." The truth was, he'd wanted somebody to love him no matter how he rebelled, but it hadn't worked that way. Maybe parents loved their kids no matter what they did, but no stranger had cared that much about the defiant, lonely, scared boy he'd been.

Her voice was gentle. "What about your parents? Did you know them?"

"Not my father." He tried to sound no more than wry. "It was a case of hit and run, I suspect. My mother . . ." Mac shrugged. "She was too young, too poor, too weak. Didn't know how to cope, I guess. It was supposed to be just for a little while, until she could get a better job, a decent place to live. I was maybe five or six. She visited at first, but visits got further and further apart." He took a gulp of the beer, which didn't have the comforting heat of good whiskey. "I've thought about looking her up, but it never seems worth the bother."

He wasn't surprised by the shock he saw on her face. "Aren't you . . . curious?"

"Why should I be?" he said coldly.

"Maybe something happened to her. Maybe she couldn't help it. Wouldn't it make you feel better to know why she quit coming?"

He'd debated enough with himself to be sure of his answer. "No. You can't change the past. She left my life too long ago for me to care one way or another anymore."

He saw her teeth close again on her lower lip as though she restrained herself. "Maybe you're right," she said finally. "I'd want to know, but maybe that's just because I like to torture myself."

The small attempt at humor worked, and he gave a twisted smile. "I have my moments." He pushed away his plate with a half-eaten piece of pizza that had lost its appeal. What he had a craving for now had nothing to do with food. It was the woman who sat on the other side of the table who made him hungry for more. He wanted to feel her soft lower lip between *his* teeth. He wanted to run his fingers through those thick, shiny strands of hair that tumbled over her shoulders. He wanted to feel the sleek strength of her body against his. He wanted . . .

Mac pulled himself up short. He wanted *her*. Was that supposed to be news?

To evade the bite of desire that would never be satisfied, he said in a different tone of voice, "I called Norm again today."

Her eyes flashed to his. "Your partner?"

"Um." Mac took another long swallow of beer and made himself say it. "Somebody must have betrayed me. There's no other answer."

Megan's forehead crinkled. "Somebody? You mean, someone you work with?"

"Have any better ideas?"

"Well, there are lots of other possibilities, aren't there? Like . . . oh, could the phone be tapped? You call all the time."

"I didn't, until this started. Anyway, we made damn sure that doesn't happen."

Her troubled gaze searched his. "Could some conversation just have been overheard? You know how you drop a remark . . ."

"Yeah." His mouth twisted. "Gee, Hal, want a drink? By the way, did you know MacClain went to ground in Devil's Lake, Oregon? Works for a guy named Jim Kellerman.''

She wrinkled her nose. "Okay. But you know it wouldn't have to be that expansive. Anyway, the alternative isn't very pleasant. To think that somebody you *know* . . .''

"Believe me, I've thought about it.'' He tasted acid in his throat and regretted the pizza. He'd damn near had an ulcer a few years before. Wouldn't surprise him if he were working on one again.

"How many people . . . ?''

"Five.'' He rubbed the knots on the back of his neck. "Unless somebody's slipped badly, only five people know where I am. They're not all friends, but close enough.''

Softly she said, "Do you want to talk about it?''

Did he want to? No. But he'd held too many silent arguments with himself. Could it be Gary? But why? What was the motive? Frank? His kid needed plastic surgery for a cleft palate. Was the insurance going to pay for it? If not, what would he do for his own son?

Hell, it was getting to the point where Mac even wondered about Norm. He'd caught himself weighing every nuance in Norm's voice when they talked, listening for that edge, that hesitation, that might be revealing.

Weary, he said, "I've been trying to figure out what it would take to make each one of them turn on me. You know the scary part?''

She shook her head.

"I can think of a good reason for each of 'em. I could probably come up with a couple. We all have weaknesses.''

Megan was frowning again. "Like?''

As much to himself as her, Mac said, "Bill Marshall likes money. Drives a Porsche, divorced his first wife and found himself a real looker. They live the high life, he dresses sharp. You know the kind. Inherited some money, the new wife is a model who doesn't do too badly, but they bought a house that must have cost half a million. Makes you wonder."

"Do you . . . do you *like* him?"

Mac shrugged. "Yeah, he's okay. We go fishing together once in a while. I'd have said he's honest— but now, who the hell knows?"

"What about the other four?" Megan asked, that small crease still between her brows.

He told her about Frank, then Gary. "I know him the least well. He's the youngest, new to our office about a year ago. Good reputation. He's married, though, and has two little girls."

"That's a weakness?" Megan said incredulously.

"If it makes you subject to pressure?" Mac shook his head. "Damn right."

Those vivid blue eyes didn't leave his as she tilted her head back for the longest swallow of beer she'd had yet. "Is that everyone?"

"Miguel Ramosa. Married but no kids. Miguel's trouble is, he can't keep a grip on his temper. Hasn't gone anywhere in the Bureau because sooner or later he makes every supervisor mad."

"You're saying he might hold some kind of grudge?"

Mac slouched lower in his chair and yanked the pull tab off his can of beer. He thought better when he had something to fiddle with. "God knows. He and I have always gotten along pretty well. But maybe he just wants to foul up an investigation. Maybe he figures he deserves some bucks for putting up with the Bureau's crap all these years. Your guess is as good as mine.''

"And the fifth one is Norm."

Mac grimaced, feeling a headache squeeze. The recurring headaches of the first few days had gradually diminished. This one probably had more to do with the burning in his belly than it did with the lump on his head.

He grunted. "Yeah. Norm. You know, I'd have said he was the unlikeliest, but by God, he knows the most about my movements. And he wants to retire early, figures he can't afford it. One little coup like this would do it."

Megan burst out, "It's horrible having to . . . to pick people apart like this! These are your friends! Like Norm. I've heard you talk to him. I know you trust him! There's no way he'd hand you over just so he could take early retirement. What if he *knew* you were thinking things like that?''

"Goddamn it!" Mac slapped the tabletop. "If Norm were the one sitting here, he'd be wondering about me!''

She shook her head hard. "I'm not so sure. There's got to be other ways you could have been found. Maybe your job has made it too easy for you to think the worst of people. Are you even considering how else it could have happened?"

Through gritted teeth, he said, "What do you think I've been doing all week?"

"Checking out local people. Which I guess made sense." The dubious way she said that grated. "But the FBI is a big government bureaucracy! Everything must be computerized. Somebody who knows what he's doing can break into any data base. And what about other people who work there, like secretaries and clerks and bookkeepers? Surely one of them would be a more likely leak.''

Mac growled, ''Do you think I'm stupid?''

She waved that off. ''Of course not. But how do you get your paycheck, for example?''

''Norm picks it up and forwards it.'' With exaggerated patience, he said, ''No, I did not let the Social Security administration know my new name and address. I don't call my next-door neighbor twice a week to see how my house looks. I haven't called a single old friend. When I said only five people know where I am, I meant it.''

''You mean, your friends don't know what happened to you?''

''Friends and family are the easiest way to find somebody on the run.''

She threw up her hands. ''But it just doesn't make sense!''

''It makes perfect sense.'' Willing his emotions to be icy, Mac met her eyes. ''The truth just happens to be ugly.''

''Having to sit around analyzing your friends for 'weaknesses' is ugly, you're right about that!''

He shoved his chair back. ''You think it's my idea of a good time?''

Her chin came up. ''Maybe not, but you're good at it!''

''It's my job!''

''To notice your friends' weaknesses?''

Anger was hot in his throat. ''I'd be a fool to trust people indiscriminately. When the hell has anybody come through for me?''

The minute the words were out, he wished them unsaid. They had come from the buried child who had painfully learned not to trust others.

But her expression had already changed. He saw compassion, tenderness that twisted his gut, and pity. It was the pity that stung.

"I've trusted all five men before with my life," he said roughly. "But things have changed, in case you hadn't noticed. My life depends on my not making a mistake. I'd be a damned fool to assume decent people can't be bought."

"You're wrong," she said, shaking her head. "It's not true! People don't all have that kind of weakness. I would never betray a good friend. Never. And I don't believe you would."

"You don't know me well enough to say that." He went to the refrigerator for another beer. Alcohol was one form of escape he usually avoided, but tonight it was the only one he could afford. What he wanted was to sweep Megan into his arms and carry her up those narrow stairs to the pristine bed at the top. He wanted to kiss her until she couldn't talk back, see the blue of her eyes deepen with desire. He wanted to bury himself in her, forget for at least a few minutes that he'd endangered her and that when this was all over he'd be walking away again.

"That's not true!" Her answer held the kind of passion that made him sure she'd respond as generously with her body. She did nothing halfheartedly— except maybe fight her attraction to him. Fight it she did, but he knew she felt it. Her face was too expressive to hide powerful emotions.

"Okay." Beer can in hand, unopened, he bumped the refrigerator door shut with his hip. "What's my greatest weakness?"

"That's easy," Megan said without hesitating. "You can't totally trust anybody."

"In my world, that's a strength."

She changed direction, startling him. "Have you ever been married?"

Mac cracked open the can and took a cold swallow. "No."

"Why?"

"Because . . ." He stopped. He'd never considered marriage, even when he was seriously involved with a woman. Why? Hell, maybe Megan was right. It didn't take a psychologist to guess that he was afraid of a replay of his mother's desertion. "Maybe being smart enough not to get married is a strength, too."

Megan smiled, her mouth curving so softly he felt a hungry kick of desire. "You're a cynic. Someday, somebody will cure you of it."

"If you're not careful," he said, deadly serious, "someday, somebody will cure you of being so trusting. The lesson'll be a bitter one."

"Do you trust *me*?" she asked suddenly. "Or do you think I'd sell you out if this, this Saldivar called?"

Yeah, if he'd ever trusted anybody in his life, it was Megan Lovell. America's sweetheart. What an irony. The funny part was, he'd trusted her even out in the lake, the scene of his worst nightmare. Her eyes had mesmerized him, her voice had been eerily calm. He had lain there like a child, giving up the iron control that had kept him whole inside all these years.

The answer to her question shocked him cold. Maybe it shocked him most because it had come without hesitation.

"No." He had to clear his throat. "I don't think you'd sell me out."

"A miracle." Her voice was light, but in her eyes

he saw a greater truth, a shift of emotion that affected him as profoundly as it had her.

"Don't look at me like that," he half growled.

"Like . . . like what?"

"You're asking for something you don't want."

Megan didn't pretend not to understand. "This . . ." her gesture took in the cramped kitchen, the dinner leavings on the table, the intimacy, "this isn't easy."

Her veiled admission made it damned hard not to take that one step to her side. It was all he could do to remember that his job was to get them out of this mess, not deeper in it.

Deliberately crude, he said, "So you've got the hots for me just because I'm here, huh?"

Her eyes flared. "Hey, you're the one who kissed me, not the other way around!"

"Fine!" he snapped. "I'll do it again, and then we can agree on how much fun it is to live together." Logical that was not, but he was past caring. He'd never pressured a woman sexually before, but there was a first for everything. His gut told him that if Megan didn't disappear soon, a hit would be made on her. And what were the odds he could prevent it?

So he took that step nearer to her, although she had shrunk back against the table.

"Don't . . ."

He wrapped one big hand around the back of her slender neck and with the other tilted her chin up. "Then stop me," he said huskily.

They stared at each other for a long, charged instant. Reflected on her face was her inner war—one she lost. He saw the defeat in her eyes a second

before she made a small sound of longing in the back
of her throat.

She couldn't have done anything more calculated
to make him lose sight of his purpose here. With an
answering groan, Mac covered her mouth with his.

The kiss was frenzied, out of control. He gripped
her hair while his other hand yanked her up against
him. He ached with need that she answered willingly. With his teeth he discovered the softness of
her full lower lip, with his tongue the slippery heat
of her mouth. He did his damndest to devour her, to
claim her so thoroughly she would never forget his
brand on her. When they breathed at all, it was
harshly, while her head fell back and he bit the
tender skin of her neck. She whimpered then, and
ran her splayed hands over his chest. He was on fire,
the flames roaring in his ears, but when he lifted his
head to capture her mouth again, he saw her tears.

Her eyes were closed, but a drop shimmered on
her dark lashes. His muscles seemed to lock and an
eternity passed while he stared down at her. God, he
wanted her . . . but not like this. Not under pressure.

She opened her eyes then, and the blue was as
bottomless as the lake that had almost claimed him.
"Mac?" she whispered.

Sickened at himself, he lowered his hands to his
sides and stepped back. "We can't go on like this,"
he said in defeat.

She didn't move, though her eyes closed again,
and she seemed to pale.

"Goddamn it, Megan! Talk to me."

"All right," she whispered. Her lashes lifted and
her gaze met his, though he could no longer read her
thoughts. Her eyes were . . . blind, he thought, as
though she didn't see him.

"All right what?"

"You win. I'll go."

So it had worked, using her own sexuality to frighten her. Why didn't he feel triumphant?

"It won't be for long," he said. No, *vowed*. "I promise I'll get the bastard. Then we can both go back to our lives the way they used to be."

"Sure," she said flatly. "Now, I think I'll go to bed, if you don't mind."

He wanted to step aside, but didn't. "You'll leave tomorrow?"

"After work." Her mouth compressed. "I'll have to make . . . arrangements. Somebody will have to take over at the beach, and . . . and I'll need to tell my parents." She gestured vaguely. "And pack."

"Okay." He did move out of her path then. "I'm sorry."

Her eyes fleetingly met his, and he felt as though somebody had punched him. She didn't bother even commenting, just swept past him.

SEVEN

The county parks department accepted the loss of
Megan without too much fuss. An old friend was
having a difficult pregnancy and was desperate for
help this last month, Megan told them, suppressing
feelings of guilt. What choice did she have but to
lie?

The next day—her last—she stayed late to tidy the
records and to leave notes in the personnel files on
each of the lifeguards. Departing, she discovered as
she looked around the empty boathouse, was easy.
Too easy. Which went to show how much she was
needed.

Mac was waiting at the car. He'd hovered close
all day, though she wasn't sure whether he was rein-
forcing last night's lesson or worried about her
safety. Well, after tomorrow he could quit worrying,
she thought morosely as she crossed the parking lot.
She would be twiddling her thumbs in a hotel somewhere, while he chased down killers.

She'd considered a long visit to an old friend from
college, who she knew would have welcomed her,

but remembered what Mac had told her. The easiest way to trace someone on the run was through family and friends. She couldn't take the chance. If he was right, if someone really did want her dead, she would only be endangering Anne. Boredom beat that.

Without comment Mac let her throw her duffle bag in on the backseat and climb behind the wheel. She shot him a glance. "Gee, are you sure it's safe for me to drive tonight?"

"Do I detect some sarcasm?" He slouched low in the seat.

"I wouldn't dream of it." Looking at him had been a mistake. Her throat tightened and she concentrated on starting the car and steering out of the lot. They drove in silence. Megan couldn't think of anything to say. Tomorrow morning would be goodbye. At most, someday she'd hear his voice on the telephone letting her know she could go home again.

Only, she had a feeling that home would never be the same refuge. Her cottage, the lake in all its moods, the town itself and neighbors she'd known since childhood, would no longer represent safety and contentment. Mac had breached both.

On impulse she took the turn from the highway onto the lake road. Mac made no comment. Because she had stayed late, dusk was almost past. Sunset was fading behind the ridge and the lake was enveloped in darkness. Still she had a sense of déjà vu. She drove carefully on the windy road, but her foot eased from the accelerator as she passed the turnoff where she had stopped that fateful night.

Mac gave her an unreadable look as her head turned. "See something?"

"That was where I was parked when I hauled you in," she said. "I guess you wouldn't remember."

"Not one of my sharper moments," he agreed.

Megan pressed more firmly on the accelerator and the car speeded up again. When she saw headlights in her rearview mirror, it struck her that there had been no other traffic. Well, no wonder. It must be nine o'clock. Even the summer residents of Devil's Lake weren't big on nightlife.

Suddenly a flash of brightness in her mirror made her flinch. "Damn it, that car has its high beams on," she muttered.

Mac straightened and looked over his shoulder. "Hell, he's coming fast. Speed up. See if you can stay ahead."

"Mac . . .?"

"I don't have a good feeling about this," he said grimly.

Apprehension grabbed at her, and Megan pushed down harder on the gas. They jumped ahead, but as windy as the road was, she didn't dare go much faster. Somehow the car behind them was still gaining. She couldn't make out its outline or color with the high beams blinding her.

They were going too fast for safety. In the next turn she heard her wheels crunch momentarily on the gravel shoulder. Here the road was high above the lake, cut into the side of a cliff. There was nowhere to go, nowhere to pull off. Megan clutched the steering wheel with hands that had begun to sweat.

In the next brief stretch of straight road the car behind made its move. "Christ, he's going to try to pass!" Mac said. "Don't let him by!"

Absolute terror held her rigid, but somehow she made herself turn the wheel sharply, cutting off the hurtling car that was trying to come abreast. It fell back at the next blind curve, then swerved again into the other lane. This time metal crunched and Megan began to pray aloud. "Oh my God, oh my God, oh my. . . ."

Another scrape of metal and she desperately held her car on the road. Out of the corner of her eye she saw that Mac had his gun out, braced on the headrest.

Slam. The Honda shuddered and skidded onto the shoulder. Megan quit even praying. This time when metal scraped it was the guardrail. Somehow they made it back onto the road. Another curve was coming, but the other car didn't fall back. "Mac!" she screamed, and he pulled the trigger.

A window shattered, then another one. Mac uttered an obscenity, fired again. The other car seemed to hesitate, then slammed into them again. This time Megan lost control. They were swerving helplessly toward the precipice. She heard herself screaming, but somehow she held onto the steering wheel. The Civic bounced off the guardrail again and miraculously back onto the road going the right direction.

The road straightened again and the other car hurtled forward. Mac shot again, deafening Megan. She looked in the rearview mirror. Bright lights. No, just one, Mac must have shot out the other. Another shot, and the pursuer abruptly lost speed.

"Got him," Mac said in satisfaction.

The drama reflected in her mirror riveted Megan. The Civic limped into a curve, but the one headlight behind didn't follow. It was still moving, as though the driver no longer saw the road. Metal ground in agony when the car hit the guardrail straight on. The beam of light pointed over the lake, then spiraled as the car flipped off the edge.

"Oh my God," Megan said again. Her foot had

involuntarily reached for the brake. The Civic slowed and she guided it onto the narrow shoulder. Though the engine still ran, the silence seemed absolute.

Then Mac asked hoarsely, "Can you back up?"

Somebody nodded—she wasn't sure who it was. She felt . . . detached. That was it. Megan put the emergency flashers on and her little Honda obligingly crept in reverse, though the steering wheel pulled. Her car would never be the same.

"Stop." When she did, he climbed out, gun still in his hand. "Flashlight?" he asked in a low voice.

Megan nodded and fumbled in the glove compartment, then handed the flashlight to him. Though her legs were shaking, she got out, too. Megan followed the tiny beam of light to the torn guardrail. The drop was sickeningly sharp, the lake black below. She stared down, thinking how easily it could have been them, swallowed by the cold dark water.

Mac walked away, his feet crunching softly on the gravel, but she didn't even watch him go. She just stood there, impossibly tired, almost numb. When he came back, he said, "I didn't think there was time for one of them to jump out, but I thought I'd better take a look."

"One of them?"

"There were two," He looked through the gap in the guardrail, then said gently, "Can you go for help, Megan? I'd better wait here."

"Help?"

He took her chin in his hand and lifted her face. The light glanced across her face and she felt his fingers tighten. Then he said in a bracing voice, "Come on, if you could rescue me from way out there, you can drive a mile or two."

She blinked. "If the car makes it."

"The car'll make it if you do."

"Okay." Docilely she turned away, but his hand stopped her.

"You did a hell of a job, sweetheart." His mouth came down hard on hers in a kiss so brief, it shouldn't have been so electrifying. Then he gave her a gentle push. "Go on. Get Pete if you can."

"Okay," she agreed again, but this time she was thinking, not just reacting. By the time she reached the car it had all caught up with her. She got back in, but her hands were shaking so badly she couldn't turn the key in the ignition. Even her teeth were chattering. She leaned her forehead against the wheel and made herself take long, slow breaths.

It was over. She and Mac had won. All she had to do was drive to the sheriff's department on the outskirts of town. How hard was that?

This time, though her hand still shook, she succeeded in turning the key and her small, battered car responded.

Hours later, Zachary barked and Megan heard a car pull into the drive in front of her cottage. She and the golden retriever met Mac and Pete Tevis at the door.

Mac's gaze took in her state of shock. "You okay?" he asked.

"I'll survive," she said. "Did you . . . did you find the car?"

"Yeah, though we still have a little problem." Something in the way he said it made her realize he didn't really mean the "little."

Oh, Lord. Had she really believed the nightmare would all be over? Megan bit her lip and stepped back. "Come on in. I'm glad you're here, Pete. Can I get either of you a cup of coffee?"

The deputy looked older tonight, his face drawn. He grimaced. "Thanks, but I've had plenty. We had a Thermos of the stuff."

Megan could still feel Mac watching her as they automatically headed into the kitchen. She had started a fire in the small potbellied stove, but it hadn't cured the chill that still made her shaky. She picked up the mug of herb tea she'd been sipping and waited until the two men sat at the round table.

"What happened?"

Mac said bluntly, "One of the two men got away."

Megan sucked in her breath.

Pete Tevis shook his head. "Pulled the car out, but only the driver was in it. Appears Mac shot him. The passenger window was open, though, and Mac insists there were two men in that car. Did you get a look?"

Quelling the panic that flipped in her stomach, Megan shook her head. "The headlights were so bright, and I had to concentrate on my driving . . ."

"You did a hell of a job," Mac said again.

"Couldn't the body have . . . have floated away?" she asked.

"Unlikely," Pete said with obvious regret. "The divers took a look around. Of course, it's black as ink down there, so they could have missed something, but a car window is pretty narrow. I'd have a hell of a time squeezing through one."

Megan turned to Mac. "Are you *sure* . . . ?"

His dark brows rose. "That there were two men? Yeah. The shots were coming from the passenger side."

"Shots?" she echoed.

Now Pete looked surprised. "You're missing a few windows in your own car out there."

"I thought that was Mac."

Mac slouched in his chair, his intent gaze never leaving her. "They were shooting back."

"Oh, God." Megan abruptly rose from the table and rushed to the small bathroom under the stairs. The soup she'd made herself eat finally decided not to come up, but she leaned against the sink and splashed cold water on her face. What was the matter with her? Why was she falling apart *now*?

Why not? she thought, half hysterically. The only reason she hadn't fallen apart the night she rescued Mac was because there wasn't time to think. Tonight she'd had four hours to sit here and remember. She had replayed every second of the battle: the scream of metal, the fight to hold on to the wheel, the sound of shattering glass, the skid toward the edge, the miraculous recovery. Over and over she saw the other car ripping through the guardrail, hanging in space for an eternity that might have been a second, then plunging down nose first.

And over and over she told herself that this had been the end. Whoever was in that car had been asking for it. She would not feel pity, only gratitude because she was alive.

She dried her face and looked at herself in the mirror. "Big mistake," she muttered, and turned the doorknob at the same time Mac opened it.

"You okay?"

"Why do you keep asking me that?"

His eyes were so dark they appeared almost black. His face was gaunt tonight, too, showing as much weariness as she felt. He grunted. "Maybe that's because you look like hell."

Megan made a face. "Just what I needed to hear."

Pete stood behind Mac, his expression compassionate. "I'd better head back to the department and see what's going on."

"You know, there wasn't any other traffic on that road," Megan said. "Even if the guy did escape from that car, where could he have gone?"

Pete nodded. "We're searching the shoreline and woods, but with no luck last I heard. If he made it as far as the highway, somebody would have given him a lift."

"Do we even know if these were the same men?"

"Yeah." Mac looked away. "I identified the one."

"But it was so dark . . . Oh." Megan felt stupid. "You mean, after they recovered the body."

He made a noise she took for acquiescence, and she suddenly realized that his weariness was probably less physical than spiritual. Looking at dead men— especially one he'd shot—couldn't be easy, even for a police officer. "I'm sorry," she said softly.

Their eyes met briefly, but the effect was searing. She blinked and wondered if she had imagined the raw emotion she'd seen.

"Megan, I'll stop by in the morning," Pete said. "See you off. You'd better get out of town while the getting's still good."

Megan nodded jerkily. "I'd better go pack. I thought . . ." She shook her head hard. "Never mind."

With the dog padding behind, she fled up the stairs, leaving the two men quietly talking by the front door. She was shaking again, she discovered as she hauled her suitcase out from under the bed. But, damn it, *she would not cry*.

Opening drawers, she grabbed piles of clothes and dumped them in the huge suitcase without sorting. Her eyes were wet, but beyond rubbing her sleeve across them, she refused to acknowledge the fact. Socks, an extra pair of tennis shoes, bras, underwear, all went in the suitcase with no rhyme or reason.

Finally she stopped and closed her eyes. She felt like a toy whose stuffing had been tugged out. Ignoring the suitcase, she slid to a sitting position on the floor, leaning against the bed. Sheer habit threaded her fingers in Zachary's coat. He was reassuringly warm, the head he laid on her lap heavy and comforting.

Beyond her fear and shock, she finally traced the root of her distress. It was tomorrow, the moment she would climb into a rental car and turn onto the highway, leaving Devil's Lake and southern Oregon behind. She had never set out on a journey and had no idea where she was going. Should she head north? South? Would she be safe here in Oregon, or should she keep going until she was in utterly strange territory?

Megan closed her eyes again and imagined herself alone, the road open ahead of her, leading . . . nowhere. Her only company would be her fear. Every car that gained on her would make her pulse jump, every driver who didn't dim his high beams, every stretch of road that was too deserted. How long would she have to look over her shoulder? Would she ever be able to stop?

Megan didn't hear footsteps on the stairs, but suddenly Mac was in the doorway to her bedroom. He propped a shoulder against the doorframe and opened his mouth to speak.

She beat him to it. "Don't ask me how I am. I'm lousy. You know it. I know it. I'm not cut out for this stuff."

"Is anybody?"

"You must be."

"I wouldn't say that."

Why she was angry at him she couldn't have said, but resentment blistered in her chest. "Aren't you the one who told me you could just pack up and leave anytime? No ties, remember? You must be looking forward to tomorrow. You can forget you were ever Ross McKenzie, whoever he was."

"What the hell is this about?" he snapped.

The fight went out of her. "I don't know," she mumbled. "Just forget it. That should be easy, right?"

She'd said too much. His eyes narrowed with sudden understanding. "I'll never forget you," he said quietly.

Her eyes were wet again. "You can if you want," she said in a muffled voice. "I don't care."

As soundlessly as he'd appeared in her room, he crossed to the bed and crouched in front of her. Strong fingers lifted her chin so she had to look at him. "Aside from everything else," he said, "you saved my life. I may be a bastard, but I'm not a big enough one to forget that. I'd do anything for you. You know that, don't you?"

She gave a jerky nod, but her agreement was a lie. She knew he would die for her, that much was true. But what she had begun to realize she needed and wanted was for him to love her. He hadn't offered love, and he never would. After hearing about his childhood, Megan wasn't sure he was capable of loving anyone.

But maybe tonight, for a few hours, she could pretend. "Mac, will you kiss me?" she asked huskily.

He made a sound that might have been torn from him, but was all the answer she needed. Then his mouth covered hers in a kiss as devastating as her emotions.

He dropped to his knees and hauled her up to meet him. Megan wrapped her arms around his neck and held on for dear life. He plundered her mouth, demanding a response she was eager to give. Her lips felt bruised, but she kissed him harder. His body was long and powerful against hers, and his erection pressed against her stomach. She whimpered and bit his lip. In answer Mac groaned, his mouth leaving hers. Before she could protest, he nipped at her neck and she let her head fall back. With one hand he tugged at her shirt, pulling it away from her jeans. Inside, he struggled with the front opening of her bra.

"Yes," she whispered, then exultantly, "Yes!" when the bra fell away and his big hand engulfed her small breast.

A moment later he untwined her hands from his neck to wrench her shirt off over her head, taking the wisp of a bra with it. Megan was shocked by the sight of his face. The angles of cheekbone and jaw seemed sharper, the shadows more exaggerated. His eyes blazed like molten iron and his mouth was twisted. He was almost a stranger, but one who looked at her with desperate hunger. Just the expression on his face was more erotic than any other man's touch had ever been.

Very gently Mac cupped her breasts, weighing them, learning their soft curves. His thumbs traced a line around her nipples. Megan tried not to move, not even to breathe. She watched his hands shape her, felt their strength. Then he lifted his head and smiled at her. In that smile she could imagine all the tenderness and desire and love she wanted to see. And so she smiled back, making no effort to disguise her own emotions.

He groaned again and wrapped his hands around her waist, effortlessly lifting her as he stood in one graceful motion. He shoved the suitcase aside, then laid Megan across the bed and followed her down, one knee braced between her legs. When his mouth closed on her taut nipple, Megan cried out and threaded her fingers in his hair. He tasted and suckled and rubbed his rough cheek against her breasts, then threaded a line of maddening kisses down her flat stomach to the top button of her jeans. Kneeling above her, Mac unfastened her jeans and drew them down her long legs. And then he kissed her there, where she was hot and wet and desperate. Her hips bucked and she pushed herself up on one elbow.

"Not fair," she protested, in a voice that didn't sound like her own.

He lifted his head and grinned. "Who said it had to be fair?"

"I did." And she sat up and with his cooperation tugged his sweatshirt off over his head. Then, nervously, she began working down the zipper of his now too-tight jeans. She was almost afraid when she saw the size of him, but he was so sleek and hard and blunt that something deep inside her cramped with longing.

Mac responded to the tentative touch of her fingers

as involuntarily as she had to his mouth. His voice sounded like gravel. "Sweetheart . . ."

"You feel so good," she murmured, and rubbed against him like a cat who wanted something.

"Damn right I do," he growled, and with his weight bore her back against the bed. The blunt tip pressed against her opening and he kissed her, tongue probing in a taste of something more primal to come. "Wrap your legs around me," he whispered. "That's it. Oh, God, that's it." And he was in her, buried as deep as her earliest memories.

It felt so good, like nothing she'd ever known. He started moving, lifting her hips, withdrawing and then filling her, the rhythm calling up responses from unlearned instincts. She heard a voice calling his name and was astonished to recognize her own. She sounded like a wild woman. She *was* a wild woman. He was silent, each thrust coming faster, harder.

The drive to the finish demanded everything she had to give. They rolled and twisted, separated and came together, the tension building until it was unbearable, until it had to explode. And then it did, in a sweet, hot tide that washed her away and left something new and different in its place. In gratitude and pain, she knew she would never be the same person again.

If kissing Megan had been stupid, making love to her was suicidal. It should have been sex, plain and simple. Hot and sweet, making a nice memory and spicing his anticipation for next time, even if the woman with her legs wrapped around him was a different one. No matter how good the sex, that's the way it had always been.

Instead, Mac felt sick with a hunger to hold her

more tightly. He lay there across her big bed with Megan's head on his shoulder and his arms around her. His skin was cooling except where it touched her. He closed his eyes and pressed his cheek against the thick silk of her hair, trying to make himself face tonight's finality. She was supposed to go one way tomorrow, he another. It was pretty damned unlikely that they'd ever find themselves in the same bed again. What was he going to do, take two weeks of vacation next summer to see if she wanted to take up where they'd left off?

Assuming he was alive—and that she was alive. If she had to hide only for a matter of days, he was confident she wouldn't be found. But what if this thing dragged on? What if weeks passed, months? Sooner or later she would use her bank card, charge something on a credit card. She'd get homesick and call her mother. She'd start forgetting tonight's terrifying events and convince herself it had really been him they'd been after. And then she'd come home. Maybe by then they wouldn't care about her, but Mac didn't believe it. A professional killer was professional because he almost never screwed up, and when he did he cleaned up after himself. Megan was a little mud on the carpet that wouldn't be tolerated.

What if she died? Died because of him? A detached part of Mac was staggered by his own emotional response. He wanted to believe that he just couldn't face the fact that she might suffer more because of him. Gut-level honesty forced him to look at the truth: He needed her. He could no longer imagine life without her.

She murmured something and shifted, not away but closer. Just like that, he wanted her again. Mac was smart enough to know his reaction wasn't totally sexual. She was his, all his, when he was buried inside her.

He swore silently. He had never wanted to kill, even though he'd done it. But tonight he would have given his right arm for both men to die. Then Megan, at least, would have been freed from this nightmare. Dead men don't care about witnesses.

There was no way he was going to let her go tomorrow. The certainty hit him as hard as a slug from a .44 Magnum. He immediately tried to justify it. The least he could do was see her settled somewhere, make damned sure the bastard who'd escaped tonight hadn't made a quick enough recovery to follow her.

He owed her. Mac didn't want to think about love. She had turned to him tonight because terror made you reach for life the next minute. That didn't mean what she felt had any significance beyond this bed. With a return to normal life, she'd want a normal guy, not one who'd admitted he hardly remembered his real name. But that didn't change what really counted here. He owed her a chance to want that normal guy.

So when she stirred and turned her head, he said softly, "You asleep?"

"Um." Her breasts pressed more firmly against his side when she inhaled before a sigh. "Just trying to . . . hold onto the moment. And not think about tomorrow."

"Well, I *have* been thinking about tomorrow."

He could feel her withdrawal, both mental and physical. She didn't move far, but an inch opened between them. "And?"

"I figure we should stick together, at least for a few days."

Now Megan scooted back far enough to raise up on one elbow. "Wait a minute. You've been trying to get rid of me."

"What happened tonight changed things. I need to hole up long enough to give Tevis a chance to identify the dead man. Then I'll know for sure who I'm dealing with."

"So you can go into your act where you're a worm wriggling on a hook."

"Yeah." He tugged so that she sprawled on top of him. "Until then, I want to know for damned sure that you're safe. The only way I can do that is handle it myself."

"Mac . . ." Despite her undignified position, Megan gravely studied him. "You should do whatever you have to. Not play bodyguard some more."

He tried to lighten the moment. "Even if the body is this good?"

"Especially then." She searched his face. "I wasn't trying to . . . tie you."

"I know." He grabbed a handful of her thick hair and pulled her face down for a long, hard kiss. Then he said gruffly, "I won't promise more than a few days, but I want to set you up somewhere, be sure you can't be found. I can leave with an easier mind then."

Her eyes closed, and she whispered, "Thank you. I was . . . scared."

"I know." He kissed her again, scared himself. Scared of losing her, scared of the tenderness that welled in his chest.

"Mac?"

"Um?" he murmured against her mouth.

"Can we take Zachary?"

A tail thumped from beside the bed, and despite

himself, Mac grinned reluctantly. "Yeah, what the hell. What's one more?"

If the dog was hoping for some more conversation, he was disappointed.

EIGHT

"How's this place look?" Mac slowed the rental car to a crawl as he and Megan gazed at the row of cabins that fronted on Lake Shasta. Zachary panted over Megan's shoulder, the heat obviously getting to him.

With late summer the water in the lake was low, exposing the dry, cracked banks of red mud. In contrast, the lake itself was aquamarine, a welcome sight on a day when the temperature was pushing a hundred.

"I guess it's okay," Megan said doubtfully. The cabins weren't prepossessing; they could have used a coat of paint and the ground in front was dusty. On the other hand, this small resort was out of the way. Megan was the one who'd noticed a faded, tilting sign out on the main road. This place was isolated enough to ensure she and Mac wouldn't run into anybody staying at a fancier resort.

"I'll go see if they have a vacancy."

Megan nodded "I'll let Zachary out for a minute, just in case we have to go on."

She watched Mac head for the office, his stride slow enough to show that he was as tired as she felt. What with one thing and another, they hadn't slept much last night, and they'd left at the crack of dawn. Mac's blue T-shirt was sweat-stained, but when he lifted his arms above his head to stretch, she didn't notice anything but the play of muscles and the sheer masculine beauty of his narrow hips and strong back. Then she looked at Zachary, who was panting nonstop.

"You're too long-haired for this climate," she said affectionately. "How about a dip in the lake?"

Somewhere he found the energy to bound out of the car when she opened the back door. Two kids who were scratching pictures in the dust with sticks lifted their heads to watch him. Megan whistled softly and the retriever followed her down a path that circled the nearest cabin to the lakeshore. The cove was a long, narrow one, with a roped-off area at the tip. Megan continued on the path to the deserted side of the cove.

It should have been cooler here, but wasn't. Boat traffic farther out made small waves, but not the faintest hint of a breeze came off the lake. Megan looked longingly at the water, but she couldn't do much more than wade until she unpacked her bathing suit. On the bank she found a two-foot-long stick and tossed it into the water. "Go get it, boy!"

Zachary hit the water with a long, arcing dive that almost submerged him. He came up shaking his head, his webbed feet slicing the water as smoothly as her crawl stroke did. Two minutes later, he dropped the stick at her feet and gave a great shake that splattered her with secondhand water. "Not the way I would have chosen to get wet," she told him sternly, snatching the stick before he could grab it in his mouth again. Back-handed, she gave it another toss. "Here you go!"

A minute later, Mac said from behind her, "Well, he looks happier, anyway."

Megan turned. "Any luck?"

"Yep. Somebody just checked out. The manager's not sure about this weekend, but we have the last cabin for the next three days anyway."

"Thank God," she said, then, in the next breath, "Are you sure we've come far enough?"

His gray eyes were narrowed against the brilliant sunlight bouncing off the lake. "I don't know that it makes much difference. There's a happy medium between the back-of-beyond and getting lost in a crowd. I figure Lake Shasta in the middle of summer fits the bill."

Megan nodded. She was just drained enough by the heat to accept any reassurance. "Any chance there's air conditioning?"

"Are you kidding? I'll be impressed if the shower works." Then he grinned crookedly. "Hey, what do you say we take a dip?"

Zachary bounded up, dropped the stick, and shook again. Water flew everywhere.

Megan laughed despite everything. "That's called asking for it."

"Obnoxious dog," Mac said good-humoredly.

Zachary reluctantly left his stick and accompanied them back up the path. Mac had already moved the car to the last cabin from the road. The door creaked when he unlocked and opened it, but the inside wasn't bad. Faded but clean green linoleum covered the floor, and the kitchenette at one end was tiny but functional. Megan couldn't help but notice the one and only bed, double instead of queen. Cozy.

She investigated the cupboard while Mac brought in the suitcases. ''There are even pans,'' she said. ''Now we don't have any excuse to eat out.''

His gaze met hers across the room. ''It's just as well if we don't.''

The reminder was an unpleasant one that chilled Megan despite the heat. She nodded and silently followed him outside to help bring in the last of their luggage, including a forty-pound bag of dogfood for Zachary.

Megan hung up a couple of shirts before she came across her bathing suit. ''I'll change in the bathroom,'' she said quickly.

Mac raised a brow, but didn't say anything.

Knowing it was silly, Megan still closed the bathroom door behind her. Lord knew he'd seen everything she had, but the passionate, impulsive actions of last night didn't keep her from feeling self-conscious now.

By the time she emerged in her Speedo suit, Mac wore athletic shorts and was just shutting his gun and shoulder holster in a suitcase that he shoved under the bed. Half of Megan hoped it would stay there; the other half was nervous that they would be stepping out the door so vulnerable. She just said, ''You're sure you want to do this?''

''Swim?'' He shrugged. ''I don't mind getting wet as long as my feet are on the bottom.''

Down at the lake, Megan dropped her towel on the bank and left her rubber thongs beside it. Then she waded in knee-deep before diving the rest of the way. The water was pleasantly cool in comparison to the heat of the afternoon. She came up laughing.

Mac still stood about thigh-deep, looking dubious. Zachary was swimming toward her.

"Oh, no, you don't," she said, fending him off as she swam a lazy breaststroke toward Mac. "Zach thinks I'm a rock he ought to be able to climb on," she told Mac. With her cupped hands, she shot him with a stream of water.

"Hey. Just remember you have to come out of this lake sooner or later, and then you're in deep trouble," he warned.

Megan laughed and emerged from the water. Now the hot sun on her wet back felt good. "Can you swim at all?"

"I can float on my back, dog paddle a little." His mouth quirked into a smile. "Though I'm not in Zach's class."

"Who is? He can probably beat me." She took a deep breath. "You want a lesson?"

Alarm subtly changed the lines of his face. "Hell, no."

"Come on, what do we have? A couple of days at least?" She splashed him again and coaxed, "I can have you swimming by then. Next time someone drops you in the lake, you can save yourself."

"That was the first and last time," he said stubbornly.

Megan admired the drops of water glistening on his sleek brown chest. "This is your big chance. Don't blow it. How many people have a chance to get taught by the best?"

A reluctant smile softened his hard mouth. "Modest, too."

She stuck out her tongue. "Just advertising my services."

Megan let him think about it while she chased

Zachary across the narrow cove and watched kids
splashing at the shallow tip that was roped off. Not
her responsibility, but the lifeguard in her couldn't
help an occasional assessing glance.

When she returned to Mac, she found him back-
floating, his eyes closed. She would have thought he
was relaxed if she hadn't noticed how tight his arm
muscles were. His eyes opened when her wave
lapped at his face and he stood up quickly.

Seeing his wary expression, Megan just said, "Hi.
Guess what? I won."

Mac glanced past her to the retriever who'd almost
reached her. "Tough on his pride," he observed.
"Maybe you'd better let him win once."

Did Mac's pride not allow him to take the chance
of appearing foolish in front of her? she wondered.
It wouldn't be surprising, considering how macho
most men seemed to be. And this one was a cop.

But Mac surprised her. "Okay. I'm ready."

"Really?"

His voice was grim. "I don't like being scared of
anything."

Megan accepted his motivation with a nod. "Can
you face-float?"

"For about two seconds, until I panic."

"Take my hands," she said, holding them out. As
he obeyed, their gazes met. Megan tried to communi-
cate reassurance, but she didn't know if she succeeded. Determination was all she saw on Mac's
face.

When she stepped back, he eased into a float, lasting considerably longer than two seconds, although
his grip on her hands was so hard they hurt. Finally
he reared up and shook his head, spraying water like
Zachary had.

"Good," she said, smiling. "Now I'll show you how to kick."

He nodded, and she recognized the same unusual quality that had made the rescue possible: an iron will stronger than any fear. She wondered if the same will could overcome emotional fears. Could he make himself take the risk of loving someone, even though in his heart he must believe he'd be betrayed yet again?

Mac made love to her that night with the same single-minded intensity he'd brought to the swim lesson. He was tender, sometimes gentle, sometimes rough, passionate to the point of desperation. With kisses he drank in her cries, but except for an occasional involuntary groan was silent himself. She knew when his body shuddered with release, but he gritted his teeth to hold any sound in.

Megan wondered about that silence and what it meant. What was it she always told her kindergarteners? Talk to each other. Don't wonder why someone is mad at you; ask. Tell your friends what you feel.

So she kissed his chest, which happened to be the closest part of him, and said, "How come you're so quiet?"

"Right now?" He sounded surprised.

"Well . . ." Now she'd gotten herself into it. "I mean the whole time. When we're . . . you know."

"Are you blushing?" He lifted her chin and his amused eyes took in her hot cheeks. "You are. What's the matter? Can't you say it?"

"What should I say?"

"We were making love." His eyes narrowed as something showed on her face. "Or isn't that how you look at it?"

"Speak for yourself," she said tartly. "I'm just not used to talking about it. I'm only a kindergarten teacher. Our school district doesn't start sex education until fifth grade."

Mac laughed. "You haven't talked about sex since fifth grade?"

Megan punched him. "You're evading the subject."

"What's the subject?"

"Why you're so . . . so quiet."

He brushed her hair back from her face with a gentle hand. "Just because I don't tell you how beautiful you are doesn't mean I'm not thinking it. You have the perfect body. Feminine . . ." He lightly cupped her breast. "Strong." His hand stroked over her flat stomach. "Just enough softness, but not too much."

That wasn't what she wanted to hear. Well, she didn't mind hearing compliments from him, but what she really wanted to know was how he felt. But she had said all she dared. She should be grateful he wasn't the kind of man who used the word love easily, trading it for sex. What if he did smile at her with that wicked, sweet grin and say he loved her? Would she believe him?

He felt her sigh. "Bored already? Jeez, lady. What's it take?"

Forget love, Megan told herself. Enjoy the moment. It wouldn't last long.

"Um." She pretended to think. "How about going skinny-dipping?"

"One lesson wasn't enough for you?"

Megan sat up and tucked her feet under her, then grabbed a pillow and very casually hugged it so that it hid most of her from the neck down. "I won't teach you a thing," she promised.

Mac crossed his arms behind his head. Tufts of light-brown hair in his armpits struck her as very sexy. And wasn't she far gone when she found armpits attractive, she thought ruefully.

"I don't know if I'm quite ready for night swimming," he said. "I kind of like to have an idea where the bottom is. Speaking of which . . ." His hand snaked out to deftly whisk her pillow away, "I don't mind keeping an eye on yours, too."

Megan gasped and dove for the pillow, which he tossed across the room. When she jumped up, he grabbed her and rolled her under him. Laughing, he pinned her down. "Hiding?"

She made a face at him. "I was being modest."

Mac kissed her, hard. "I like you better when you're being immodest."

She began, "I'm never . . ." but he kissed her again and her hands crept up around his neck.

When he lifted his head, Mac was breathing hard, and Megan had forgotten what they were arguing about. "Like that," he said roughly, and kissed her again.

"What we need," he announced the next morning, "is someplace that sells books."

"And a toaster," Megan mumbled, as she stirred the scrambled eggs and waited for hot water to boil before she could have a cup of coffee.

"A little under the weather this morning?" he asked with infuriating good humor as he pulled a T-shirt over his head.

"I never get enough sleep when you're around."

"I didn't hear you complaining."

She wrinkled her nose and started dishing up the eggs. "Well, now I am."

Mac's voice dropped a note, becoming husky. "Remind me tonight."

"Right," she said, knowing how likely that was. Megan poured two cups of instant coffee and then plopped the plates of eggs and bacon on the small dinette table just as Mac sat down. "Lunch is your turn," she announced. "And we really need some more groceries."

"Like I said," he agreed, "we can find a store. As long as it has a decent selection of reading material. Not that you bore me . . ."

She melodramatically clasped her hand over her heart. "Surely not."

He grinned, his face utterly relaxed, his eyes downright friendly. He'd changed, Megan thought, as though he had set aside his internal guards when they fled Devil's Lake. Was he usually like this, when life was a little less stressful?

The coffee helped unfog Megan's mind right away. "What do you do for fun when you're home?" she asked out of the blue.

"Read." Mac swallowed some coffee. "Take in a baseball game. I play city league basketball. Run to stay in shape." He shrugged. "I'm in one of those Big Brother programs. I have this kid named Raul, who's a real hellion. We've gotten along okay since I pounded him at one-on-one. He couldn't believe somebody so old could still put a move on him."

Megan nibbled on a piece of bacon. "Does he know where you are?" she asked softly.

Mac shrugged again as though indifferently, but he also turned his head and gazed out the small-paned window at the lake, the hot mug of coffee cradled in his hands. "I . . . let him know I'd be gone for a while. He understands."

"You sound like you miss him."

The crease in one cheek deepened. "Yeah, I guess I do. God knows why. Half the time his mother calls me to bail him out of hot water. He cuts classes, gets caught smoking in the hall . . . His dad's in the state pen for armed robbery. But you know, Raul's a good kid. Despite everything, he keeps a B average, says he's going to college. He's stubborn. I'm betting he makes it."

With Mac on his side, Megan would bet on it, too. Assuming Mac could ever go home again. She wondered if Raul missed him, if he was cutting more classes because Mac wasn't there to nag him, if he'd be tempted to do something stupid with a group of friends because Mac wasn't there to care. Part of her had been wishing this small idyll would last forever, that she and Mac could just linger here, responsibilities to others forgotten. But the picture her mind had formed of Raul, mouth sneering and dark eyes full of hero worship, killed her secret reluctance to face the future.

She had a life to return to, too. Even if she suspected it would never be quite the same.

"Can we really go grocery shopping?" she asked.

"Hm?" Mac turned his head to look at her, his expression abstracted. She wondered what he had been thinking about. Remembering. On a stab of apprehension, she wondered for the first time if there was a woman, back in that other life.

She bit her lip and studied his face. "Did you have a girlfriend?"

His eyes sharpened. "What brought that on?"

It was her turn to shrug with pretended indifference. "Your expression."

He grimaced. "Did I look like I was pining away?

No. I haven't had a 'girlfriend' in a while. My job tends to make it hard.''

"Did you ever think about quitting?"

"Frequently." He took a bite. "What's with the questions?"

"I don't know," she said honestly. "I guess this is just the first time we've had a chance to, oh, seem normal. I'm sorry. I don't mean to be nosy."

"I don't mind." He smiled, reminding her suddenly of one of the monstrous little boys in her class who looked sweet while planning something awful. "Gives me a chance to ask the same questions."

Megan pushed her plate away. "Is there anything you don't already know about me? Maybe what brand of toothpaste I buy?"

"Oral-B. Bubble gum flavor, no less. I put away the groceries last time, remember?"

"I like it," she said defensively.

"Yeah, sure." There was that grin again, sexy and dangerous. "Must be undue influence. You spend too much time with five-year-olds."

Megan stuck her tongue out at him.

Mac saluted her with the coffee cup. "I rest my case."

"Can we drop it and talk about something important? Like whether we can go grocery shopping?"

"Sure we can. After you answer the rest of my questions."

What did she have to hide? But for some reason she felt like a teenager in her first job interview. She slouched more comfortably in the padded booth and tried to look nonchalant. "Okay. Shoot."

His intensity showed even while his tone was lazy. "How come no boyfriend?"

"Would you believe, not much choice in Devil's Lake?"

"No."

She looked away. "I'm not exactly Miss America. Men aren't lined up to break my door down."

Megan sensed a change in the atmosphere even before Mac leaned forward and said tautly, "Do you know how badly I wanted to splinter your damn door every night? You can't tell me I'm the first man who has felt like that."

Her smile wavered. "Yeah, I can tell you that. I mean, I dated in college. But lately? I have lots of friends who are men. None of them even knock on the door."

"Bullshit."

"True." She made herself meet his gray eyes. "When I was a teenager, I wasn't flirting with boys. I was staring at a black stripe in a swimming pool. I think I missed a stage in there. Flirting 101. I just don't know how to do it."

"Sweetheart." Very deliberately Mac put his mug down and levered out of the booth to stand. He held a hand out to her. She let him tug her out of the booth, somehow ending up half sitting on the table with Mac standing between her legs. "Sweetheart," he said again, "you do it just fine. Trust me." He bent his head and kissed her, his mouth lingering. Then he lifted his head and said huskily, "I'd give you an A."

The constraint she'd felt miraculously lifted, and Megan was able to respond in kind. "What I want to know is, what do *I* have to give you to get that A?"

"Um. A little of this . . ." his hand cupped one

breast, "a little of that . . ." the other hand stroked down her throat. "We'll figure something out."

"Oh, good," she breathed.

"Do we really need to go grocery shopping?"

"Only if you're desperate for a good book."

"I think we can put it off." Mac unexpectedly lifted her, and Megan grabbed hold, wrapping her arms around his neck and her legs around his waist. "For an hour or two." He kissed her, then smiled. "Too bad the table's covered."

"Ever seen *Bull Durham*?" she asked provocatively.

His rakish grin flashed. "I don't want to pay for the dishes."

"Oh, well." She tried to look disappointed. "I guess the bed will do."

"We'll replay this scene," he murmured as he nuzzled her ear. "After dinner. Once we've washed the dishes."

"Good," she whispered, and let her head fall back.

Mac drove right past the big Safeway and found an out-of-the-way Mom-and-Pop store. Prices were higher there and the reading material consisted of used paperbacks, but he felt safer. He settled for a couple of thrillers and some westerns, and somehow wasn't surprised when Megan chose historical romances. He'd known from the beginning that she was a closet romantic; not the kind of woman you messed with unless you meant business. So what excuse did he have?

They swam again, to Zachary's delight. Mac face-floated and kicked for close to twenty feet. When he shook water off his head, he said, "Hey, Teach, what d'ya say?"

"Very good," Megan said in a sugary voice. "You know what? I think you're ready to learn the arm stroke."

"You mean, we get to the real stuff?"

"Right." Her full mouth curved into a smile that offset her stubborn chin.

Mac watched half seriously as she leaned forward to demonstrate a crawl stroke that even his inexperienced eyes recognized as long and smooth. Trouble was, her bathing suit was hardly decent, which had a way of distracting him. He'd noticed that lifeguarding she had worn two, one over the other. Now he knew why. Wet, the thin fabric of the racing suit clung to her supple body, showing nipples that had tightened the minute she hit the water. The damn suit was cut high over her hips, which were almost—but not quite—boyishly narrow.

Hell. Why did this one particular woman push his buttons so hard? *Hard* being the operative word, he thought ruefully. Well, he never had liked lush and overblown, in women or anything else.

He also had a suspicion he was focusing on his physical attraction to Megan in part to keep his mind off the rest of it. He could handle lust after a woman; wondering if he could live without her was another matter.

"Now you try it," she said, and he obediently leaned forward and immediately felt inept as he tried imitating her movements. "Good," she said, "just get your elbows a little higher. Reach out in front. Like that. Very nice."

Patiently she took him through the strokes. She coaxed and soothed until he was confident enough to add the arm stroke to his face-float. Mac didn't tell her about the panic that clutched him every time the water closed over his head. He tried opening his eyes, knowing the darkness was part of his fear, but the lake water was so murky that didn't help. He'd never been crazy about water in any quantity; hell, maybe he hadn't liked being trapped in his mother's womb. Whatever. Perhaps swim lessons when he was eight years old would have cured him. But he didn't get them, and now he was thirty-two. Worse yet, somebody had tried to kill him not so long ago by dropping him into deep, dark water.

And he had to fall for a woman whose natural element was water. Who was insisting he start rhythmic breathing.

"If God had meant man to breathe in the water, he'd have given us gills," he muttered.

"I think he did and we just got tired of them," Megan retorted.

"Why don't we save the breathing for another day?" Mac suggested. "My book, my lawn chair, and a cold beer are calling me."

Megan splashed him. He splashed back. Somehow he ended up carrying her, slung over his shoulder, out of the water. She was shrieking and he was enjoying the view of her rear end, just rounded enough.

"Make you a deal," he said, when she came close to wiggling out of his grip. "We call it quits now, and I'll take you skinny-dipping tonight."

She stilled, and he could hear the smile in her voice. "Deal."

Hell. Now he'd done it. He didn't just have to go swimming, he had to do it in water dark as midnight.

"Are you sure nobody else is down here?" Megan whispered.

"I don't see anybody."

"I can't see any*thing*," Megan said.

"Then nobody'll be able to see us, right?" Mac's low, amused voice made her feel prudish. And this had been her idea, for heaven's sake.

"Ow." She stubbed her toe and hopped a couple of steps. Once the trail passed out of the scattered trees, moonlight added visibility, and Megan could make out the line of dark shore and glass-smooth lake. Considering it was midnight, she wasn't surprised that not a soul was in sight.

In front of her Mac dropped a towel on the beach and began to disrobe. Gulping, Megan did the same.

Moonlight silvered Mac's skin, accentuating shadows and the lean play of muscles. Megan hesitated, threw off her T-shirt and said quickly, "Race you in!"

The evening had cooled the air to nearly the same temperature as the water. The sensation of passing from one element to the other with so little contrast between was eerie. The water slid over Megan's bare skin, and she stretched and rolled her shoulders as she dove porpoiselike beneath the surface. She surfaced and turned back to the dark shape that must be Mac.

"It feels good," she said, hearing her own surprise.

"You've never done this before?"

"Nope." She lazily breaststroked toward him. "We used to talk about it sometimes. Maybe climbing over the fence into the pool at night, but we never actually did it. It wouldn't have been the same anyway. A pool is so . . . artificial."

"Yeah, and you could have turned the lights on." Under his casualness, Megan could hear tension. The memory of that night and the endless dark water didn't disturb her, because this was where she belonged. Swimming had always been a primal pleasure to her. She'd sometimes fancied that she did have gills, that she had been made to live her life in the water. As a child she had often felt so clumsy out of it.

"You don't have to come in if you don't want," she said repentantly. "This was probably a dumb idea."

"Nah." He lowered himself into the water. "It's better to face things that scare you."

"Um." She slipped around behind him and wrapped her arms around his shoulders. "A little company never hurts."

"What scares you?" He turned so suddenly she lost her grip and floated free.

Megan half sat, half treaded water with her hands making easy figure eights. The moon was behind Mac, so she couldn't see his face. Something made her decide on honesty. "You do," she admitted.

A moment of silence greeted her admission, and she wished desperately that she could read his expression. Then he said abruptly, "You scare the hell out of me, too. I thought you were a mermaid the first time I saw you. Something out of a fantasy. I thought I must be dead."

"Is that why you didn't fight me?"

"I figured I was dead either way. You looked more pleasant than the alternative."

A small shiver cooled her skin. She'd thought of the alternative, too. "I'm sorry," she said. "We shouldn't have come."

"I don't know. This isn't so bad." Then, surprising her, he lay back and floated. She followed his example, looking up at the moon. Unexpectedly,

Mac's hand came out and found hers. Megan returned his grip, grateful for a small peaceful moment. For the first time in weeks, all fear left her. She didn't even let herself think, only revel in sensation: the strength of his fingers, the brush of air against her skin, the weightlessness water gave her, the moon and the night.

NINE

While Mac talked at the pay phone, Megan waited in the car. When he at last emerged from the phone booth and walked toward the car, she knew.

She waited until he climbed in behind the wheel and slammed his door. "The dead man's been identified."

"Yeah." Mac wrapped his fingers around the steering wheel and looked straight ahead through the windshield. "Renato Mendoza. He's been connected with Saldivar before."

"So now you know."

"I knew," he said, still not looking at her. "Now I have to do something about it."

Megan, too, gazed ahead, watching without really seeing the traffic passing on the highway. The phone booth was outside an Arco gas station. She tried to sound calm, collected. "Do you want me to stay here, or should I go somewhere else?"

When Mac didn't answer, she turned her head. He was looking at her, his brows drawn together in a frown, his expression brooding. "Damn it, I don't know what to do with you."

"What do you mean?" she retorted. "I'll do what you wanted me to in the first place."

"I don't like the idea of you off by yourself."

He said it so brusquely, she couldn't feel flattered. "What, you think I'm going to do something stupid?"

"I don't know," Mac snapped. Then he sighed and rubbed the back of his neck. "No, I don't think you'll do anything stupid. You're scared enough now to behave yourself for a while. But damn it, it's so easy to screw up."

"Maybe," she agreed, puzzled by his rare indecision. "But what choice is there? For you to keep playing bodyguard?"

"Let me think about it."

"Do *I* have a choice?" she asked tartly.

"No." He turned the key in the ignition and took advantage of the first opening in the traffic to pull back onto the highway.

Not knowing whether she was angry or hurt, Megan sat beside him in silence. He had changed so quickly, from the relaxed, passionate lover she awakened beside this morning, to the guarded, even cold, man she had first known. Which one was the real James McClain?

Why did he feel differently about her being alone now? Was it because he knew her better, thought her impulsive, maybe? Or was it because he cared more about what happened to her? Megan wanted very badly to believe the last. She knew, though, that she might be kidding herself.

It was late afternoon when they made it back to the cabin. Zachary hopped off the double bed when Mac unlocked the front door. Even though they had left the curtains drawn, the small cabin was uncomfortably hot. Megan was sweating, her hair sticking to her neck. She headed straight into the bathroom to brush her too-thick brown hair into a ponytail. When she came out, Mac was lying on the bed, both pillows shoved behind him. His hands were clasped behind his head and he gazed broodingly at the wall in front of him.

"Do you want to go swimming?" Megan asked.

He gave her a distracted glance. "Not right now."

"I'm going by myself, then," she said, turning on her heel.

When she emerged from the bathroom again, this time in her suit with shorts pulled over it, Mac frowned. "Where are you going?"

"Swimming," she said shortly. What had happened between them? Why had they reverted so easily to their antagonistic relationship?

His tone was flat. "I don't want you going by yourself."

Megan bristled. "Why not? What do you think I'm going to do, drown?"

"I just want to know where you are."

"Well, you know," she said, grabbing a towel off the back of a chair and flinging open the outside door. "Come on, Zachary." The retriever bounded after her.

She knew she was behaving badly, that he had good reason to be worried, but the way he snapped orders infuriated her. What was she supposed to do, stare at the wall with him? Why bother, since he'd made clear that she had no say in whatever decision he made?

Megan swam back and forth across the cove, Zachary valiantly trying to keep up. She'd done ten laps when she saw, not at all to her surprise, that Mac had followed her down. He wasn't swimming, just sitting on the baked, red-orange slope that rose from the water. Ignoring him, she swam another ten widths before she left the water. Megan picked up her towel and wrapped it sarilike around herself, tucking the end in.

Mac watched, his expression distant. Megan studied him, trying to imprint his image in her memory. High forehead, cheekbones that gave his face angles and planes, hooded gray eyes and a mouth that could be cruel or tender. The lines between his dark brows were more obvious than usual, the grooves in his cheeks carved deeper. He could use a shave and his dark-blond hair was shoved back without a semblance of style. He should have been suavely handsome, and instead was pure male.

She felt as if a tourniquet had been tied around her heart.

With a sigh Megan sat beside him, wrapping her arms around her knees. This time she looked at the lake, turquoise-blue, and the speedboats making crisscrossing plumes. "I'm sorry," she said, her voice constrained. "I was just . . . frustrated."

He nodded but didn't answer.

"Have you decided what to do?"

"Up to a point. It's time to bring this thing to an end. No more hiding. I want it done, one way or another." He grunted. "That's where I run into trouble. I need help, but I don't dare trust anyone who can do me any good."

"Your partner . . ."

"Could have sold me out," he said harshly.

"Now wait a minute." Megan touched his arm. "I don't think you really believe that."

Mac shoved his fingers into his hair. "I don't

know what the hell to believe. The first thing I should do is put him to the test.''

"Do you really need to do that?" Megan asked. "Has he ever let you down?"

His chest rose and fell on a long sigh. "No. But this time my safety isn't the only thing riding on my judgment.''

"Are you talking about me?"

"Damn right."

Without hesitation, she said softly, "I think in your heart you do trust him, or you wouldn't have kept calling him regularly. And I trust *you*."

Mac turned his head sharply and their eyes met. She saw shock in his before he looked just as quickly away. There was silence for a moment, and then he said brusquely, "So be it."

She nodded and sat quietly beside him. At last she had to ask. "What about me? What should I do?"

"You know," he said, with seeming casualness, "I may pretend I'm bait, but I don't intend to get eaten.''

Eaten. Shuddering, Megan remembered her first glimpse of Mac, the two men shoving him overboard like a bundle of garbage. Could she bear it if something like that happened again, and she was off hiding her head in a hole?

"Would I be in your way?" she asked.

He didn't look at her. "I don't see what difference you'd make, if you're willing to follow orders."

The decision wasn't hard. "I'd rather stay with you.''

Now he did turn his head. Their eyes met, his so clear a gray she could have tumbled in and sunk without a trace. "I shouldn't let you," he said, "but I was hoping you'd say that.''

Megan let out a breath she hadn't known she was holding. "Then . . . what do we do next?"

"We call Norm." He rose to his feet and held out a hand. "No time like the present."

Half an hour later they had found another phone booth. Mac wouldn't take the chance of using the resort office phone. "We're damn careful, but with technology changing as fast as it is, somebody might come up with a new way of tracing a call. I don't want to be found until I've issued the invitation."

Megan wasn't sure she wanted to be found then, either. On the other hand, as Mac had pointed out, what was the alternative? Living on the run?

She waited in the car this time, too. On the way back to their cabin, Mac summed up the conversation.

"Norm's traveled the same route I have. It's got to be one of the other four agents. He's done a little asking around, figuring what the hell. They all know my troubles. They're not stupid. They'll have come to the same conclusion."

"Must make for congenial working conditions," Megan muttered.

"Yeah."

"And?"

"He hasn't gotten any interesting answers. Didn't find any big debts. The only one with a lifestyle out of step with his income is Bill Marshall. I told you about him."

"The one who married the model."

"Yeah. Well, Norm managed to find out how much the inheritance was. It nicely paid for that fancy new nest."

"Then . . . where do you start?"

"Ramosa is in hot water again. He's gotten his

wrist slapped so many times, this round they're suggesting he find a new career."

"Do you really think . . . ?"

"Goddamn it, *somebody* is behind this shit!" Mac snapped. "Don't start in on me."

Megan's voice rose. "I wasn't . . ." Then she made herself take a deep breath. "I didn't mean that the way it sounded. I'm just asking for . . . your opinion. That's all."

There was silence for a moment before she saw him rotate his shoulders as though in answer to the same kind of tension she felt. "I'm sorry," he said roughly. "I don't like any of this. I shouldn't have taken it out on you."

She swiftly touched his arm. "It's okay."

He took one hand off the steering wheel to cover her hand, but didn't say anything.

After a moment Megan said, "So you're going to start with this Ramosa."

"It's a case of eenie, meenie, minie, moe. Norm says he's damned bitter. My gut tells me it's not him. My head isn't so sure."

Megan only nodded. "So what's the plan?"

Mac told her. It sounded so simple. Norm would find a way of letting Ramosa know where Mac was. Mac and she would actually rent a room elsewhere, as well as a second car, and stake out the cabin which they'd leave looking occupied.

If nobody came hunting them, in six or seven days they would move to a new location and Norm would drop the word to the second suspect. Then they'd wait again.

Sooner or later, as Mac said, someone would take the bait. It was the waiting that would be hard.

*　　*　　*

In the days that followed Mac changed. Maybe she did, too, Megan wasn't sure. But the easygoing man who teased her, whose voice was amused as often as it was husky with passion, had turned into someone else. During long stakeouts of their beachfront cabin he was endlessly patient, silent for long stretches, his few comments brief to the point of taciturnity. When she tried to argue about the vantage point he'd chosen to watch the cabin from, he wouldn't rise to any bait.

"This is best. With the angle of the morning sun, nobody'll see us."

"But it's uncomfortable," Megan said, hoping she wasn't whining. "Couldn't we move behind those trees . . ." But he wasn't even listening.

When they weren't watching the cabin, Mac was physically restive; while she read or watched TV, he would prowl the small confines of their hotel room. The few times he let her swim at a deserted cove, he waited on the beach, his watchful gaze traveling nonstop over the shoreline and boats that approached within half a mile. Megan felt as if she was accompanied by one of those blank-faced Secret Service men she'd seen on TV, who always seemed to wear dark glasses to hide whatever vestiges of emotion remained.

Oh, he made love to her, but differently, almost grimly. The night he decided it was time to leave Lake Shasta was typical.

They had found a hotel room in a big place just off the highway and rented the second car, while ostensibly holding onto the cabin and the first car. There was no way they could keep the cabin under surveillance twenty-four hours a day, but Mac spent ten to twelve hours every day watching it. Catching the hit man wasn't the object, as Mac pointed out;

the fact that an attempt on their lives was made at all would put a name to the traitor in his office.

"But I sure wouldn't mind catching this SOB, too," he said, in a voice that chilled her.

Usually Megan went with him, but sometimes he left her in the hotel. Those times alone made her nervous, and she thought he felt the same, that there was relief in his eyes when she opened the door at his voice.

It was nearly ten that night when he returned. He sank wearily onto the queen-size bed and said, "They'd have shown up by now if they knew where we were. It's time to make our next move."

"Could they have been watching and . . . and guessed we weren't really there?"

"That's always possible, but I don't think so. I've driven in and out, ducked out of the back door, turned lights on at different times. The place is busy enough that they wouldn't take a chance of being seen peeking in windows." Mac shook his head as he stripped his grey sweatshirt off. His voice was muffled by the shirt. "Saldivar's not a patient man."

"We can't stay here?" Megan asked uncertainly. It should have made no difference to her where they were; Lake Shasta wasn't home territory anyway. But it had become familiar and, therefore, safe. She knew the beaches, the grocery stores, the highway. Change was always scary. She'd known too much of it.

"You know we can't," he said, hardly glancing at her. "When somebody strikes, we've got to be damned sure where the leak was. If we stuck around here, how could I be sure whether Ramosa or the next guy had passed our locale on?"

She didn't argue. What was there to say? Megan didn't even ask where they were going.

"We'll turn the first car in," Mac said. "Make sure we're not followed. We can rent another when we get there. I think we'll head over to the coast. The resort here was perfect. I want to find another one like it."

She knew what he meant. He'd liked the fact that their cabin was separate enough from the others that nobody else was likely to be hurt accidentally. It scared her even more than she'd already been, to be in love with a man who assessed hotel rooms by how vulnerable they were to attack instead of how comfortable the bed was.

Silently Megan went into the bathroom and brushed her teeth and changed to her nightgown. When she came out, Mac gave her one comprehensive glance, then without comment went into the bathroom himself. By the time he came out, she was already in bed, her reading lamp turned off.

She was tired, bone-tired, and desperate to be held. Not in passion, but for comfort. She wanted reassurance, understanding, tenderness. And she wanted them from Mac, who was as tired as she and unlikely to understand her needs.

She heard the shower running, and at last Mac came out of the bathroom naked except for a towel wrapped around his waist. His hair was wet and spiky, and though he had obviously shaved, weary lines were carved deeply on his face.

He turned off lights as he came, finally settling heavily down on the edge of the bed, where he tossed the towel onto a chair and pulled the covers up. Mac switched off his bedside lamp, and in the darkness

Megan thought for a minute that he wasn't going to touch her at all.

Then he turned suddenly and slipped his arm under her neck, gathering her in. On a sigh she snuggled up to his warm strength and closed her eyes, glorying in the feel of his embrace. His other hand brushed hair back from her face.

"Sitting around waiting is hard, isn't it?" he said in a low voice.

She was surprised that he'd read her mind. She nodded, knowing he could feel the motion.

"It's not so different from anything else you're not looking forward to," he said. "You just want to get it over with."

One way or the other. The phrase popped into her head, but she stayed silent. She didn't even know what most frightened her. Was it herself she feared for? Or Mac?

"I need to kiss you," he said gruffly.

Megan lifted her face willingly. Mac's big hand framed it, and then his mouth found hers unerringly. No gentleness here, she recognized immediately. Perhaps this raw desire was the masculine counterpart to her own need for simple contact. Whatever drove him, she responded to. Her lips were bruised, her tongue took part in a duel, his teeth bit her neck sharply enough to hurt for a fleeting instant. But something feminine in her reveled at being the object of such desperate hunger. This wasn't the way a man took a woman who didn't matter; this was the way he made love to one he was afraid of losing.

He entered her almost roughly, too, after wrapping her legs around his hips and gripping her buttocks in large hands that held her steady as he thrust deeply. She cried out, as much in pleasure as shock, and

Mac's fingers clenched tighter as he held himself still with an effort that had him trembling.

"Please," Megan whispered.

"Stop?" She hardly recognized his voice.

"No." She ran her fingernails over his back. "Make love to me."

It was as though she'd unchained him. He groaned something she thought was her name, and then drove hard into her, again and again, faster, deeper. Sex had always been a mutual coupling, pleasurable but not an act that branded her as his. This time, she thought with what little part of her that could still reason, he was claiming her.

And at the end he did something else he never had before. He gave a guttural cry that could have been ripped out of him just as he shuddered with the shock of climax.

Afterward Megan held him as he lay heavily on her. His muscles were slick and hard under her caressing hands. He didn't roll away as he usually did, and she was glad.

How many more nights would they have? she wondered. If they survived this trap Mac had set, then what? Would she ever see him again?

The Oregon coast was as beautiful as Megan remembered it. She hadn't been here in years. The narrow highway climbed on cliffs above the Pacific. Thickly forested land ended abruptly in the rocky cliffs, and stacks worn by the pounding waves stood sentinel out in the ocean.

Right now Megan could just see a gravel beach below, the cove protected by the arms of forested points, one crowned by a white lighthouse. The day had begun gray, with mist curling over the highway

and softening the outlines of passing cars while dull-
ing the deep green of fir and cedar. Megan was glad
that they were going north instead of south. She
wouldn't have wanted to be too close to the guardrail
and the abrupt drop-off. Her memories of the battle
to stay on the Devil's Lake road were too fresh. If
someone tried the same thing here . . .

She wouldn't let herself think about it.

"I'm getting hungry," she said instead.

Mac glanced at her. "If the fog would burn off,
I'd suggest a picnic."

A mileage sign appeared out of the mist, reminding Megan of a childhood holiday. "Have you
ever been to Florence?" she asked.

"Italy or Oregon?"

"Oregon."

"Nope. Anything special about it?"

"Sand dunes," she said dreamily. "Miles and
miles of them. Golden sand that slips through your
fingers and your toes. You can go sledding as if it
were snow, except it's warm. I must have been eight
or nine the time we went there. I loved that
vacation."

"Many places to stay around there?" Mac asked.

"I don't know," she admitted. "I think we
camped the time I remember. I'll bet there are,
though."

"Makes as good a destination as any, then."

They had a brief lunch at a fast-food restaurant,
and by afternoon had reached the small town of Florence. Mac drove around for nearly an hour before
he found a resort similar to the one at Lake Shasta,
with a vacant cabin set off far enough from the others
to satisfy him.

"Told the guy we wanted our privacy," he said,

getting back into the car. "We can spend the night here, find another place and a second car tomorrow. Want to go jump on some dunes?"

"Can we?" Megan asked, her heart lifting.

"What the hell. The dog'll need some exercise anyway."

The mist had finally lifted, though the day was nowhere near as hot as it had been at Lake Shasta. Megan changed to shorts and canvas tennis shoes, bringing Zachary's leash. The plump, cheerful woman who managed the run-down cabins offered them a plastic disk to slide on, which Megan accepted.

At the state park they joined hordes of other tourists, who were dragging everything from cardboard to surfboards up the steep dune above the parking lot. A small lake was a vivid blue-green against the golden sand.

Mac climbed out of the car, looking dubious. "You're really going to slide down that, huh?"

Megan's smile was a challenge. "And so are you."

"Yeah, right." He glanced down at Zachary. "You don't want to do that, do you, boy?"

Zachary bounced and gave one woof.

"Traitor."

Megan chuckled and hooked her hand around Mac's solidly muscled arm. "Come on. Don't be stuffy."

The climb was hard work, with the sand slipping from beneath their feet on each step. Poor Zachary lunged forward and slid back. He was panting and his long pink tongue dangling out of his mouth by the time they reached the top.

"Hell of a view," Mac admitted. The lake below shone like a jewel, and in the other direction dunes rolled like windswept waves toward the ocean, marked only by the wheels of dune buggies.

Megan climbed onto the blue plastic disk and clutched the rope handle. "You can get on behind," she said.

"I can, huh?" Mac's unenthusiastic tone was belied by the amused tilt to his mouth. "Trying to relive your childhood, lady?"

"Why not?"

He shrugged and sat down behind her so that she was between his knees. She didn't mind her position at all. "Let her rip," Mac said, and gave a shove with one hand.

The next thirty seconds were exhilarating. Zachary leaped along behind them, barking all the way. They soared down the dune, sometimes going sideways, bumping and lurching until they hit the bottom and went flying. Megan picked herself up laughing.

"Again?"

"God, I'm too old for this." But Mac was grinning, too. He ruffled Zachary's head. "You game, dog?"

They ended up making the trip four times. Megan was exhausted and briefly, shatteringly, happy. She struggled to hold onto the mood as they found a little grocery store and stocked up, then investigated the cabin's cooking facilities. Mac made love to her again that night, tenderly this time, silently.

By morning his mood had changed again, and he seemed remote. When Megan headed for the shower, Mac pulled on a windbreaker. "If you want to put breakfast on, I'll go find a phone and call Norm," he said tersely.

Megan nodded and watched him leave. When he returned twenty minutes later, she put the plate of pancakes she'd made in front of him. "Who this time?" she asked.

"Gary Mercer. He was new in our section about a year ago. The few times I worked with him he seemed okay. But he's more of an unknown quantity than the others, which makes me nervous."

Megan just nodded. What was there to say? And she was afraid that anything she *did* say would make Mac defensive. He was right; they had to do this. It must be worse for him, because he knew these men.

Except, she reminded herself, that he'd been a target before and coped. *He* was a law enforcement officer, used to doing dangerous things. She was a kindergarten teacher.

They left most of their stuff spread around, taking only an essential change of clothes and some of the food. They found a hotel room as they had the time before, then rented a second car so they could come and go.

Mac figured it was too soon to expect company; even if the guy who'd escaped at Devil's Lake had stuck around, *and* word of their new location had gotten to him quickly enough, it was a fair drive over to the coast. Back at their hotel, the evening was another long one.

The next morning, Mac made sure the manager and residents of some of the other cabins saw them ostensibly returning from breakfast, in case anybody asked questions. They were able to slip out the back door unobserved and find a place not fifty yards from the cabin where they could watch from behind a screen of salal and wild cherries. One boring hour stretched into another, but nobody stirred except guests in other cabins who came and went. Megan had to admit their cabin looked like somebody was home. Mac had left the filmy curtains drawn, so the inside was dim, but a light was on and a window was open to let in a breeze. The car was parked close in front, and a radio played softly inside.

By seven o'clock that evening Megan was numb. They had eaten nothing but sandwiches, potato chips, and doughnuts all day. As darkness approached, Mac left her several times to circle the cabins. Compared to the way he melted into the dusk, she felt like a hippopotamus crashing through the brush when she had to find a private spot to answer the call of nature.

Returning, she almost tripped over Mac. His wry glance took in her rumpled, dirty, stiff self before he resumed watching the uneventful scene below.

She dozed briefly, despite the discomfort of uneven ground and weeds that poked at her clothing. When she awakened, it was completely dark.

Megan ran her fingers through her ponytail and sat up, stretching. Blinking to clear her eyes, she said, "You can't see anything. Why are we still sitting here?"

Mac was just a dark shape, but she saw his movement as he glanced at the illuminated dial of his watch. "I suppose we might as well give up," he admitted, his voice low. "Not a damn thing has happened."

Megan nodded and felt around in the darkness for the remnants of the food they'd packed. She didn't ever want to look at another potato chip again. Fresh green beans, she thought. A peach. Broccoli. A nice crisp salad.

A few rustlings beside her indicated that Mac, too, was collecting himself. Megan stood up and brushed leaves and dirt off her jeans and sweater. "Ugh," she muttered. "You sure know how to show a lady a good time."

"Indiana Jones I'm not," came Mac's rejoinder.

Megan wasn't so sure, but she didn't argue. All she wanted was bed, and for once she didn't care whether Mac was in it or not. She gave a last wistful glance at the faint glow of lights in the cabin below, and started to turn away.

That was when the cabin exploded in a blast of orange heat.

TEN

"Hell."

Mac snatched his gun from its shoulder holster and took off toward the cabin, bent low so he didn't stand out too obviously from the dark background.

He knew damn well that he was too late. Flames crackled as the old, dry cabin collapsed into itself. In the ghostly orange light of the blaze, people emerged from other cabins to stare aghast at the inferno his had become. Just to be sure, Mac circled behind the cabin, then around the entire resort. He didn't find a thing.

How in God's name had the bastard slipped in without Mac seeing him? Making his way back toward Megan, he decided it didn't really matter. The trap had succeeded, object accomplished. Even if he didn't like the results.

Megan stood right where he'd left her, apparently mesmerized by the flames. When he touched her arm, she jumped.

"Invitation accepted," he said grimly.

She bit her lip and nodded. Mac wrapped an arm

around her and steered her toward the back road where they'd parked their car.

He opened the passenger side and gently pushed her in. She'd already buckled her seatbelt when he got in behind the wheel.

He was calculating, planning, making decisions, so her voice startled him. "Shouldn't we stay so the authorities know we weren't in the cabin?"

"They'll find out soon enough," he said. "The longer the world thinks we're dead, the better."

"Most of my clothes were in there."

"You can buy clothes."

"I shouldn't have left so much."

"It looked better that way." He answered patiently, knowing that she clung to small regrets as a defense against shock.

"Did you register us under our real names?"

"No." Mac backed the car out of the dark turn out. "And we didn't leave any I.D. The police aren't going to be able to figure out who was staying there. They'll decide it was a drug deal gone sour or something of the kind. Nobody died, it'll be forgotten."

"Do you suppose the resort was insured?" she asked anxiously.

"Yeah." Mac stepped harder on the gas. Megan needed the kind of comfort he couldn't give her on the road.

She surprised him then with a long silence. She still hadn't spoken when he parked the car next to the wing of the modern hotel where they'd taken a room. Then she said, "So now you know who it was."

"Yeah," he said implacably. "Now I know."

She didn't look at him. "What will you do?"

"Call Norm, for starters. He can pick Mercer up before he has a chance to do any more damage."

"This didn't help my situation, did it?"

Mac reached for her hand, which felt cold. "Not yet," he admitted. "If we're lucky, Mercer's met some of Saldivar's people. Maybe he knows the right one."

"Will you talk to him?"

"Yeah," he said again. "Tomorrow morning, we find a nice kennel to leave Zachary at, and you and I are heading for Miami."

Mac felt like a stranger when he walked into his own office. Some beefy guy who'd been shipped in to take his place was tilted back in the swivel chair, his loafer-clad feet smack in the middle of the desk blotter, his ear glued to Mac's phone. Norm stood in front of a file cabinet, hunting for something.

Mac leaned against the doorframe and crossed his arms, waiting. Norm was the first to glance up. "Well, damn," he said. "Look who's here." Then he grinned and shoved the file drawer shut. "Welcome back."

"I wish I was back," Mac said, straightening. "I think this is just a reprieve."

Norm slapped him on the back hard enough to jar his teeth. "Coffee?"

Mac said some hellos before they headed down the hall toward a conference room. Then he went straight to the point. "Did you get him?"

Norm was a tall, rangy man, gray replacing the brown of his close-cropped hair. His suits always fit as if he'd just lost ten pounds. He stopped dead in the hall, ignoring a couple of women who glanced at them as they passed.

"Did I get him? You think I'm incompetent or something?"

Mac grinned. "Okay, let's try it another way. Has he told you anything interesting?"

Norm sobered immediately. "Yeah. It was his wife and kids. They grabbed them all just a couple days before that hit was made on you. They've let the kids go, kept his wife. He talked to her every other day on the phone, hadn't seen her in a month. This morning she was dropped off in front of their house. I don't know how he's hidden the strain."

"So he didn't have a lot of choice," Mac said thoughtfully. He wanted to stay angry, but how could he? Not so long ago he wouldn't have fully understood the choice Mercer had made. Now he did, which made him wonder if he needed to find a new career. No, scratch that. He *knew* he needed to find a new career.

"What else?"

"He had a couple of contacts, who never admitted Saldivar was behind the grab. He met only one face-to-face. Mercer didn't let on that he knew who the guy was, but he recognized him. Enrico Silva. Ring a bell?"

"The name does. I don't know him."

Norm said, "Well, I have a picture of him. We'll see if he looks familiar."

Then he opened a door and let Mac enter ahead of him.

Gary Mercer sat at the long conference table. His elbows were on it, his head buried in his hands. He didn't look up at the sound of the door opening.

"Mercer," Mac said flatly.

Mercer looked up at last, but Mac wouldn't have recognized him if he hadn't known who was sitting here. His blue eyes were bloodshot, his face ravaged. "You really are alive,' he said.

Mac dropped into a chair on the other side of the table. "I'm alive," he agreed.

"Jesus." Mercer buried his face again.

"Where are your kids?" Mac asked.

"My mother's." The answer was muffled.

Mac looked at the man with deep pity. He was about thirty, a life full of regrets and what-might-have-beens ahead of him. He sure as hell wouldn't be an FBI agent. Mac didn't like to think about what choice he would have made in the same situation. He didn't want to find out.

Norm sat casually on the edge of the table. "Your wife's all right."

Mercer's head shot up. "You mean, they called?" he asked in obvious alarm.

"No. She's home. Saldivar played fair. You told him what he wanted to know, he gave her back."

"She's . . . they didn't hurt her at all?"

"Nope. She's here. I'll let you see her in a few minutes."

The man's eyes closed, and this time when he covered his face with his hands it was to hide his tears. Mac didn't look at his partner, just waited.

Mercer pulled himself together faster than Mac would have given him credit for. He wiped his tears off on his sleeve and looked at Mac with a face twisted by emotion. "I'm sorry."

"If you want forgiveness from me, you have it," Mac said.

"What else could I do?" the young agent pleaded.

Mac took a long breath. "I don't know," he said honestly.

"I'd do it again," Mercer said.

Mac just nodded.

Norm said, "We're still talking over how to handle this. For now we'll move you and your family to a safe house. On one condition."

Mercer visibly braced himself. "What?"

"That you testify against Enrico Silva."

Bitterly, he said, "You don't have to blackmail me to do that."

Norm inclined his head. "Good." He stood and said, "Your wife's across the hall. Are you ready to see her?"

The chair clattered as the other man shoved it back. "God, yes."

Norm raised a brow, then glanced at Mac. "Take a look at the stuff in that folder."

For the first time, Mac noticed one lying on the table. In the vacuum left by the two men's exit, he reached for the manila folder. When he flipped it open, an eight-by-eleven picture lay on top. His stomach clenched in instant reaction.

One of the two men who had tried to kill him at Devil's Lake was dead. Enrico Silva was the second.

Megan waited what seemed like hours for Mac. She tried to read, but discovered on page 52 that she couldn't remember a thing about the story. She ordered lunch from the hotel's room service, but lost her appetite when it arrived.

What was he *doing*? she wondered in frustration, for the tenth time, as she paced to the windows and back to the bed. Couldn't he at least *call*?

At 1:47 she heard his key in the lock. When he stepped inside, she was waiting in the middle of the room, trying to look composed.

He smiled tiredly. "Bored?"

"A bundle of nerves is a more accurate description," she admitted.

"I'm starved."

"What happened?"

He grimaced. "Mercer's in custody. They kidnapped his wife, held her hostage to ensure his cooperation."

"Oh, Lord," Megan whispered. "What will happen to her?"

"She's safe. Apparently Saldivar and company think we're dead. They're going to be in for a nasty shock." Mac bent his head to kiss her. His tenderness assuaged some of Megan's tension. When he lifted his head, he said, "One good thing. Mercer fingered the other man who tossed me in the drink. We're trying to pick him up right now."

Megan sank down on the edge of the bed. She knew her mouth was probably hanging open. "You mean," she said slowly, "if he's arrested, I can go home?"

"Yep." His answer sounded a little flat, devoid of the emotion that should be there. "Your problems are over."

"But yours aren't."

"Not unless we can talk Enrico Silva into testifying against his boss. Frankly, he'd be a fool if he did."

"But he'll go to prison for years if he's convicted of trying to kill you!" she protested.

"He'll be dead if he fingers his boss."

"What about that program where the government helps people hide?" she asked.

"The Federal Witness Program?" Mac shrugged and headed for the telephone. "We'll try to talk him into it. Unfortunately, it's not a very appealing alternative. For one thing, sometimes people get found anyway. The only way to disappear once and for all is to forget who you were. That means never seeing family or friends again, changing your career, your hobbies, maybe even your face. And you can't let your mouth run away with you. Ever. Too often, people can't stand it. Sooner or later, they make a mistake."

"Like you were afraid I would."

His gaze was level, unrevealing. "Yeah."

When she didn't respond, he turned away and picked up the menu that lay beside the phone. She watched him yearningly, knowing how close her time was to running out. With that matter-of-fact description of a life on the run, he had awakened her own fears. He sounded so clinical, as though it were just a matter of being careful. She had almost forgotten their early conversations.

"Would you do it?" she asked. "Instead of going to prison?"

He glanced at her. "Hell, yes. But remember, I don't have any family. I'm used to going undercover. Being chatty isn't one of my problems."

Troubled, Megan nodded and didn't say more. She could feel his gaze on her. Finally he asked, "Hungry? Shall I order you something?"

"I guess," she said without much enthusiasm. "Maybe a turkey sandwich."

Mac nodded and picked up the phone. With his voice as background, Megan grabbed her hairbrush and began tugging it through her uncooperative hair. Sitting on the edge of the bed, she could see herself in the vanity mirror. She was paler than she had been, despite the swimming at Lake Shasta. Her dark hair needed a trim, she decided, and a little makeup wouldn't hurt anything. Trying to distract herself, Megan wondered if she should stop at a department store on her way to the airport; with half her wardrobe and most of her toiletries and makeup blasted to smithereens, she needed to start from scratch. Or maybe she could spend the night in Portland before she caught the bus for Devil's Lake.

Because she had no doubt she would be going home. After all, even if Mac felt anything substantial or lasting for her, what could he offer her now? He was probably already busy making up a new identity, deciding where to settle this time while he waited for something that might never happen.

And wasn't home what she had wanted most?

"I should make you a plane reservation," he said suddenly, harshly.

Megan bit her lip, then nodded.

His voice was rough. "Megan . . ." But a knock at the door interrupted him.

By the time he'd tipped the bellboy and seen him out, Mac seemed to have thought better of whatever he had intended to say. He watched Megan finish braiding her hair, then said, "Come and eat."

She still didn't have any appetite. *And I should be relieved!* she thought in despair. Her safe, orderly life had been given back to her. Now was too late to discover that it no longer mattered most.

To keep Mac from noticing her withdrawal, she went over to the small table by the sliding-glass door where he had laid out the food. "What are you going to do this afternoon?" she asked, proud of how detached she sounded.

"Right now, wait for the phone to ring," Mac said. "If Silva is back in Miami, he shouldn't be hard to find. He's a real professional, careful enough so he doesn't need to hide. No police department has ever had the evidence to arrest him, even though his name is well known.''

"Careful," Megan repeated. "That's one way to look at it."

Mac's gray eyes were perceptive. "Yeah. Saldivar sent him because I'd have recognized most of his men. Silva's a free-lancer. He's done work for Saldivar before, but he keeps personal contact to a minimum. So I never had occasion to meet him when I was part of the organization."

Megan nodded again. Curiously, she asked, "Was it hard, pretending to be . . . like them?"

A flicker of some emotion crossed his face, but he answered dispassionately, "Not as hard as you'd think. It's a business, and they look at themselves as businessmen. They have a product, distributors, suppliers, accountants."

"And murderers."

"Yeah, but you have to understand. That's not how they look at themselves. That's the hard part. I'm the law; we're moralists. If you even let yourself *think* about moral judgments while you're under, you're dead."

Megan knew exactly what the scar on his belly looked like. "Is that what happened to you?" she asked.

His mouth twisted. "No. It was just bad luck."

Megan felt as far from understanding him as she ever had. How could he *not* make moral judgments?

He was familiar, and yet a stranger. Extraordinarily handsome, with strong cheekbones and patrician nose, a sexy mouth and hooded gray eyes. Yet he had never quite fit at Devil's Lake, never would, she thought. It wasn't the hair that was too long or his clothes or even the shoulder holster that he wore so casually. No, it was his guarded expression, his cynicism, his loneliness, that meant he would never be the kind of man she had always imagined she would marry someday.

Maybe those very qualities were the reason she loved him. Maybe because she, too, had a core of loneliness that nobody else had ever touched.

The strident ring of the telephone made her jump. Mac's eyes didn't leave hers as he answered the phone before it could ring again. "Yeah?" He made some noises of agreement, said he'd be there in an hour, and finally hung up.

"He's in custody," Mac said.

"Will he talk?"

"Not so far. I plan to see if I can't change his mind."

Megan felt like a puppet when she nodded again.

"Aren't you going to eat?" he asked.

"I'm . . . not really hungry," she admitted.

Silence stretched too long between them. At last, sounding awkward, Mac said, "Will you wait for me?"

Megan tried to smile. "Why not? I can leave in the morning just as well."

Mac swore and shoved his chair back from the table. Almost roughly he pulled her up and into his arms. Unshed tears burned in her eyes as his mouth claimed hers with shattering thoroughness. Megan wanted to melt, to surrender whatever pride held her backbone straight, but Mac released her too quickly. "I'll be back," he said hoarsely, grabbed his jacket and was gone.

Megan sat on the edge of the bed and cried. She cried because she had no choice but to get on that plane tomorrow, to go back to her beachfront cottage and her family and her class full of eager five-year-olds. She would have given anything, anything at all, to throw that all over and stay with Mac.

She cried most of all because she knew he wouldn't ask her.

It was six-thirty before Mac let himself into the hotel room. He found Megan packing. Sacks and sales slips lay all over the bed.

"You went shopping."

"I'd have gone crazy if I hadn't done something." She didn't seem to want to meet his eyes, but she picked up a bulging bag and handed it to him. "I bought you some stuff. I thought maybe you'd be too busy."

He glanced in. Jeans. His size, she must have looked. Two sweatshirts, gray and dark green. On top was a black T-shirt that he lifted out.

"Batman," he said, and laughed. "Appropriate, I guess. Although God knows I'm no superhero."

"You're good enough for me," Megan said, finally meeting his gaze.

The black depression that had hung over him all day returned full force and he let the T-shirt and bag fall back to the bed. "Yeah, well, this'd make a hell of a movie," he said. "The audience likes a resolution. This story seems to be running on and on."

"He won't talk."

"No surprise," he said wryly.

Megan searched his face with those extraordinary blue eyes, and Mac felt as transparent as ice. As brittle, too.

For the second time today the telephone rang, but this time he swore. "Now what?"

Megan answered it before he could cross the room. "Hello? Oh, Mom."

He had been forgotten. Mac sat in one of the armchairs and watched, unnoticed, as Megan talked to her mother.

"Did Bill pick up Zachary? The poor baby. He didn't want us to leave him. Um hm. Yes, I have a reservation. My flight gets into Portland at twelve-fifteen. I figured I'd just catch the bus." Pause. "You don't have to do that. It won't kill me . . . Bad choice of words, huh?" He saw her struggle to hold back tears. "Are you sure? I love you, Mom."

Mac tuned out when she started talking about clothes shopping. A moment later she hung up and reached for a tissue, firmly blowing her nose. Her eyes were still damp when she turned her head. Mac tried hard to look expressionless.

"Is something wrong?" she asked.

So much for his ability to dissemble. His mouth twisted into a painful smile. From somewhere words came that he'd never meant to say. "What if I asked you to leave with me, right this minute? Would you go?"

"I . . . What do you mean?" she asked carefully.

"I love you," he said. "God, I love you. I let myself imagine what it would be like to have you there every day. Which was pretty damn stupid. Because it wouldn't work, would it? You belong back home, safe and sound."

Megan walked right up to him and gently touched his cheek. Mac turned his head to press a rough kiss in her palm.

"I'm not a child, you know," she said steadily. "I left home a long time ago. I want to spend my life with the man I love, not my parents.'' Standing on tiptoe, Megan brushed her lips across his.

For a moment Mac stood immobile beneath the caress, disbelief mingling with astonished hope. Could she possibly mean what he thought she did?

"Megan," he said. Tried to say. Somehow it came out like a desperate gasp for air. But words no longer mattered, because he'd hauled her into his arms and was kissing her with the deep, hungry passion that burned in his belly all the time.

He had to have her; physical possession seemed to be the only way he could feel sure of her. Part of him knew that this time lovemaking was a way of running away. They should talk. He should make himself rationally think about tomorrow, figure out whether there was any hope of making this work.

The rest of him didn't want to listen. She was his right this second. That was what counted—it was *all* he could count on. Tomorrows had a way of letting you down.

But he didn't want to go too fast. Those times after making love to her, when he lay with her head resting on his shoulder, his skin cooling as the heat inside subsided, was when he started to think. Right now, he didn't want to think.

So he kissed her until she was weak in his arms, until her taste was his own. He laid her on the bed and stripped her just slowly enough to draw out the anticipation, and he didn't mind at all when she took her time undressing him. Nothing had ever been sweeter, he thought as he kissed her neck and then her breast, eased his fingers between her legs where she was slick and hot. *For him.* Mac's satisfaction at her response was as powerful this time as the first. When he entered her with one thrust and she cried out and held him tighter, that satisfaction became triumph. *Only for him.*

Somehow he held himself back, took it slow, let the tenderness be stronger than the hunger. She didn't close her eyes, just watched him. He kissed her and she smiled dreamily. "I love you," she murmured. "Don't make me leave you."

The knowledge that he'd have to do just that whispered at the edge of his consciousness. To drown it he kissed Megan again, harder, more desperately. She was his. Right this minute she was his. To hell with tomorrow.

ELEVEN

Megan awakened slowly, dreamily, a rare sense of physical well-being mixed with the memory of happiness that wasn't quite concrete. *Mac*, she thought, then remembered on a flood. He had said he loved her, asked if she would go with him. *Anywhere*, she thought joyously, and opened her eyes.

But the other side of the bed was empty, the rumpled covers and indented pillow the only sign that he had been there. Apprehension grabbed at her throat and she sat up abruptly. Then she saw him.

Already dressed, Mac stood by the window looking out. His back was to her, so that she couldn't see his face.

"Mac?" she said uncertainly.

The moment he turned and she saw his closed expression she knew that last night's dream was only that. Mac had no intention of taking her with him.

"Mac?" she said again, hating the pleading note in her voice.

"It wouldn't work," he answered her unspoken question gently. Implacably. "I should have kept my mouth shut."

Megan was only vaguely conscious of her nakedness and tangled hair. All of her was focused on this man who had changed her life from the moment she wrapped her arms around him in the dark water of the lake. His hands were shoved into the pockets of his khaki trousers, where she could see that he had made fists. His neck was tanned and strong above the unbuttoned opening of a dark-green henley shirt. Hair damp, he gave the impression of being collected, shielded, any emotion contained so thoroughly that she could never touch it.

"I love you," she said, desperation swallowing any pride.

His jaw muscles knotted, but his level gaze didn't change. "I was a fool last night. I'm a hunted man. Until that changes, you don't belong with me. You're safe now. Go home. You and I, we were a pipe dream, anyway. I'm not the kind of man for you. Being thrown together in danger narrows your view of the world. Give yourself a few weeks and take another look."

Some instinct made Megan pull the bedcovers over her bare breasts. As though modesty meant anything now. "And if my view of the world doesn't change?" she asked, her voice thick with unshed tears.

"I might give you a call. When my troubles are finished."

"If they ever are."

"Yeah. If." He swung away, then, and stood again with his back to her, looking out the window at the courtyard and swimming pool below their balcony. "Your flight leaves in two hours." He spoke roughly. "Norm'll take you to the airport once you're packed. I took a chance coming through there once. I don't want to run into anybody I know.''

If last night had been a dream, this was a nightmare. Megan sat there cross-legged, knowing that nothing she could say or do would change his mind. Would she ever see him again? Find out how his "troubles" had ended?

On a choked sound of despair she fled to the bathroom. There she turned on the shower as hot as she could stand it. She let the spray hit her face, and cried. It was nearly half an hour before she could collect herself enough to begin the mechanical routine of getting dressed and drying her hair. She wished she were so drained she couldn't feel at all, but wasn't that lucky. Agony welled so painfully in her chest, it was all she could do to make herself open the door and face Mac again.

If Mac was still here.

He was. He'd finished packing his own things and started in on hers. She stood in the bathroom doorway for a moment and watched him cutting tags off her purchases and clumsily folding them. She must have made a sound because he looked up.

Neither moved for a painful instant. His gray eyes were dark, the lines of his face taut. She knew suddenly that he wasn't saying goodbye to her as casually as he wanted to pretend.

"Norm will be here in a minute," he said, straightening. "I thought I'd help . . ."

Megan nodded, biting her lip until it hurt. "I'll finish," she said abruptly.

Mac retreated. "Megan . . ."

But a knock on the door interrupted him. He swore under his breath, but went to answer it. "Who's there?"

She couldn't hear the response, but Mac released the chain and opened the door. Megan closed her eyes and prayed for the strength to maintain her fragile composure, then turned to face the man who had held their lives in his hands.

Rangy, graying, he was older than she had expected. He looked as if he'd been sick, paler than he ought to be in the Florida sunshine and a little too thin.

"Megan Lovell." He smiled and held out a big hand, which she accepted. He squeezed and released her smaller hand. "It's a pleasure. I'd have recognized you anywhere, even though you've changed a little. What was it they always called you in the headlines?"

"America's sweetheart," Mac contributed from behind his friend. He was distant again, somebody she barely knew.

Her fingernails bit into her palms and she said, "That was a long time ago."

Norm's smile faded. "But you can still swim. I'd be stuck with a new partner if it weren't for you."

"That was my job. I've rescued a few eight-year-olds, too."

"They didn't weigh a hundred and eighty pounds. Hell, I know how Mac feels about water. He was probably fighting you all the way."

Megan's gaze collided with Mac's again. She said slowly, "No. No, he was . . . very cooperative."

"You don't say. Well, you ready to go?"

"Not quite." She nodded toward the open suitcase. "If you'll just give me a minute . . ."

Megan finished packing in less than a minute. Behind her, she heard the two men talking.

"You going to stay here?"

"No," Mac said. "I'd better move around. Damn, I wish I could go home, but I don't dare."

"You haven't gotten used to other pillows by now?" Norm asked genially.

"Ah, it's not the pillow." When Megan turned around, her smallest bag in one hand, Mac looked past his partner, directly at her. His mouth curled into a half-smile that didn't reach his eyes. "After that sleeper couch of Megan's, anything feels like the Hilton."

Matching his tone was one of the hardest things she'd ever done. "You should have said something. I have an extra layer of foam rolled up in the closet."

"The hell you do."

A little guiltily, she nodded. That first night she'd been too resentful of his presence to make any extra effort, and she'd just plain forgotten after that.

"We'd better go," Norm said. He sounded so gentle, she had a feeling he was reading between the lines.

"Yes." Megan blindly turned and picked up her purse, slinging it over her shoulder. "All right."

"Megan." When she turned, tears hot in her eyes, Mac had crossed the room and stood just behind her. His wide shoulders blocked her from his partner's sight.

She looked up at him mutely, and he said in a low voice, rapidly, "Megan, there's no other choice. Damn it, you know that."

In her heart, she did know. But would a promise be asking too much? Was he not making one because he was afraid he wouldn't live to keep it? Or because he thought that in the end *she* would let him down? Did Mac really believe she would see him differently once she didn't need him to protect her?

"Goodbye," she said. "Will you at least call me someday, so I know?"

He groaned, bent his head and kissed her. For a moment she forgot where she was, surrendering to the sensations: his mouth hard on hers, the texture of his shirt under the hand she'd automatically raised, the warmth beneath the shirt, his breath on her wet cheeks when he lifted his head.

"I'll call," he said roughly, and stepped away.

Norm had her suitcase, so Megan picked up the smaller bag and went, without looking back.

"No," Mac said, and stared down his boss on the other side of the desk.

"Goddamn it, McClain . . ."

"How many months is it that I've already wasted? Three? Four? And the bastard found me anyway. I've done enough running. It's time to end this thing."

Norm had the other chair in the office, though he'd remained silent until now. "We have Silva," Norm reminded him. "He doesn't owe Saldivar any loyalty. He's a smart man . . ."

"Too smart to talk." Mac shook his head. This conversation was a rerun. "As things stand, he'll serve a few years in prison, be back in business. There won't be any business if he doesn't prove now how discreet he can be."

"Sooner or later, something will break."

"We've tried that way," Mac said flatly. Later would be too late for him. Maybe he was a fool to think he had a chance at a future with Megan, but he *knew* there wouldn't be any future if he had to run forever.

"So what do you have in mind?" Mac's superior

asked. "Do you plan to take out an ad in the *Herald*?"

"If that's the best way to get word out," Mac agreed coolly. "We've played the waiting game long enough. He wants me badly. We can use that. You know how he feels about failure. His pride'll be hurt. If Saldivar has a vulnerable point, his pride is it. Let's set him up, and make sure it works."

"And if it doesn't?" his boss asked.

Like a kid playing cops and robbers, Norm pointed at Mac and clicked with his tongue as he pretended to pull the trigger. Mac didn't let his expression show any change. He just waited for the silence to end.

At last his boss nodded abruptly. "Okay. Maybe you're right. Maybe we have screwed around long enough."

Mac leaned forward. "Then let's make plans."

"This time, let's bring some more people in on it. I've stayed in touch with the Miami police on this, and I think the DEA can help us. They both want him as badly as we do."

"You'll set up a meeting?"

"For tomorrow, if I can get everybody together that soon."

"Good," Mac said fiercely.

At a knock on the frosted-glass inset of the door, Mac's superior raised his voice. "What is it?"

Bill Marshall opened the door and stuck his head around it. "We have a big problem," he said, in a voice that had Mac and Norm rising to their feet. Bill's gaze went straight to Mac. "Megan Lovell's been kidnapped. Her mother just called."

Megan had spent the flight replaying in her mind the last days and weeks, knowing it was pointless but unable to stop herself. Would Mac come to her when Saldivar was stopped?

At least she knew now that he loved her, but in the end that might not be enough.

She wondered if he really believed that for him she was willing to walk away from everything that had ever been important to her. Remembering her stubbornness those first days after she rescued him, she couldn't blame Mac if he didn't believe her. It amazed even her how utterly she had changed. She had been so certain her life was satisfying! And now?

Now it would be empty. Unseeing, Megan gazed out the small window beside her seat. Her cottage—it would be hardest to bear, because every room was imprinted with memories of Mac. The meals they had cooked and eaten together, the bathroom where his towel had hung beside hers, the living room where he slept—she hadn't even stripped the sheets off the sleeper couch, she thought. Her bedroom . . . She drew a shuddering breath. How could she go home?

School would be starting in . . . It took her a moment to calculate. Four days. Other years at this time, she had been excited, planning eagerly, reading the files on her new students. Now she couldn't seem to recall a single name.

Megan leaned her head back and closed her eyes. All she knew for certain about the weeks to come, was that the tension of waiting would never leave her. Every time the phone rang, she would answer with breathless fear, afraid to hear the worst.

She was bone-tired by the time the plane landed in Portland. Her father was coming to meet her, but she'd arranged for him to pick her up at an airport hotel in the morning. She had intended to finish replenishing her wardrobe, she remembered. She wasn't in the mood anymore, but she was glad she didn't have to face him immediately. Perhaps by morning she would have come to terms with herself and be ready to hide some of her desolation.

Once her flight landed, Megan exited the plane and collected her baggage. With only her purse, a small case, and the one large suitcase that rolled on wheels, she dodged the porters and headed for the doors.

Outside with the usual chaos: cars parked and double-parked while passengers unloaded or loaded luggage and kissed drivers hello or goodbye. Taxi drivers honked and several hotel shuttles were departing. Megan stood for a moment, disoriented. Real life with a vengeance. She wasn't ready for it.

Ahead she saw a taxi, a departing passenger leaning in the window to pay off the driver. She tugged on her suitcase and hurried toward it.

Behind the taxi was a blue sedan she scarcely noticed. Two men had gotten out and were passing her on their way toward the doors into the terminal. When one of them bumped her she said an automatic. "Oh, I'm sorry," and didn't really even look at him.

That was her mistake.

Before she could even react, Megan's arm was grabbed and she was hustled toward the blue car. "Hey!" she protested, just before she was stuffed into the backseat.

"Wait a minute!" She scrambled toward the opening, but it was blocked by a large, dark-suited man who slammed the door. "Let me out!" She pounded on his shoulder and tried to shove past him. Her only reward was the sound of the trunk closing, presumably on her luggage.

"I'm very sorry," the man said, and slapped a hand over her mouth and shoved her down.

Megan fought for all she was worth, but fruitlessly. The car moved smoothly away from the curb and joined the slow traffic passing the terminal. A moment later, it picked up speed.

The man released her mouth. "You can sit up now if you want."

She was shaking and gasping for breath. Instead of docilely settling back in the seat, she grabbed for the door handle on the opposite side of the car from the man. It was locked.

Before she could find the lock, his hands closed around her wrists and he shoved her back in the seat. Out the window she could see that they were moving fast now anyway—too fast. She would die if she jumped from the speeding car.

Her breath came in little sobs as she sank back against the seat. For the first time she looked at her abductors. All Megan could see of the driver was close-cropped dark hair. Another man was in the front seat: short black hair, a business suit, and dark skin. The one beside her, although larger and somehow tougher-looking, matched in all essentials. All three were Chicano, or Mexican, or Cuban.

If anything, terror tightened its grip on her throat. Saldivar. They must work for Saldivar.

"Why are you kidnapping me?" she asked, in a voice that shook only slightly. "I don't understand."

The man riding in the front seat beside the driver turned his head and raised a skeptical brow. "No? I think maybe you could guess."

"If this has something to do with the man I rescued from the lake . . ."

"Special Agent James McClain."

"I didn't see the men who tried to kill him. It was getting dark . . ." She had to swallow. "I couldn't possibly identify them."

He shrugged. "We don't care about that."

"Then . . . then what?"

"You're bait," he said bluntly. "We're guessing that McClain won't take a chance with your safety."

"You mean I'm a hostage."

"Yes. You have nothing to fear if the man you were foolish enough to resurrect is willing to pay his debt to you."

"You'll let me go."

"Yes. You're of no interest to us. Well," he smiled amiably. "That's not quite true. I must admit to personal curiosity about you. A pretty young woman like you, yet you must have ignored the boys to live in the swimming pool. What made you?"

Oh, God! Megan thought, knowing she was on the verge of hysteria. He wanted to discuss her past as a competitive swimmer! But hadn't she read that if you were kidnapped it was a good idea to make your captors like you?

She knew that advice was probably aimed at the hostage of some nut who'd gone over the edge, not cold-blooded businessmen who wanted to converse. But surely even they would be less likely to want to kill her if she'd been cooperative.

So she said, "I don't really know. I just . . . felt like I belonged in the water from the time I started lessons. Sometimes I wanted to quit, but . . . the reasons for quitting were never as strong as my desire to swim."

His very dark eyes scrutinized her. At last he nodded. "Interesting. Tell me, was it hard to rescue such a large man?"

She swallowed again. Her mouth felt too dry to talk, but she answered anyway. "Yes. If it had been much farther, I might not have made it."

"So the location wasn't badly chosen. It was just bad luck that you of all people happened to be there."

Now she was supposed to critique how good a job a couple of hit men had done! This was insane. Or was she the one who had gone around the bend?

"That's true," she agreed, trying to sound grave.

Those dark eyes studied her for a moment longer, and then the man turned to face the front. He said something to the driver in Spanish, and Megan glanced out the window. They seemed to be leaving the city. She saw a road sign that said Beaverton. If they went into any town, there would surely be stoplights.

Out of the corner of her eye she located the button that released the door lock. If the car began to slow, if she could move quickly enough . . .

She never had a chance. The car exited the freeway, but the man beside her grabbed her hands and pushed her face down onto his thigh. Megan wriggled and fought, but his powerful hands held her effortlessly. When the car did stop, she would have rolled onto the floor were it not for his grip.

But her mouth . . . He couldn't hold her hands and her mouth at the same time. Megan drew a deep breath and screamed.

Almost instantly she was drowned out by rock music. "Born in the U.S.A." Surely passersby would wonder about a car full of dark-suited businessmen listening to Bruce Springsteen at a deafening level! Wouldn't they look? Remember it later?

Still she fought the hands pinioning her. And screamed. Her throat was raw from her screams. She was rocked back as the car began to move again. They stopped at another light, accelerated again, and this time picked up speed. After a nightmare few minutes, the man released her.

"Don't waste your breath," he said coldly.

Megan pushed herself up to a sitting position, as far across the seat from the man beside her as she could get. The highway had narrowed, and beyond barbed wire fences were green fields.

"Where are we going?" she whispered.

The man in the front seat barely spared her a glance. "We've rented a house. It will do, while we wait."

Wait for Mac, Megan thought. Wait for him to offer himself. For her.

She had no doubt at all that he would come. A stranger in a hospital bed, he had said, "You save a life, it belongs to you. So what are you going to do with mine?"

Now she knew. The rescue had been futile. For her sake, Mac would die anyway. He would do it to save her, but something told her his sacrifice also would be futile. These men, who had allowed her to see them, would never let her go.

_____ TWELVE _____

Four hours later, Mac's rage and fear hadn't abated at all. He slammed his fist down on the desk hard enough to make coffee cups jump. "I should have seen this coming! Damn, I know the man. Why didn't I expect—"

Norm interrupted him. "How could you have predicted this move? Megan shouldn't mean anything to Saldivar."

Bitterly angry at himself, Mac leaned his head back and closed his eyes. "He kidnapped Mercer's wife. She didn't mean anything to him, either. When something works, he uses it again. I should have seen it coming."

"What could you have done, hidden her forever?"

He opened his eyes to stare savagely at his boss. "If I had to."

"How'd the snatch happen?" asked the man from the Drug Enforcement Agency who'd joined them.

"I thought her parents were picking her up at the airport," Mac said, leashing his inner frustration. "Turns out, she decided she'd like a day in Portland on her own and changed arrangements. I guess she just intended to grab a taxi. Not that it would have made any difference either way. They'd have gotten her sooner or later. Anyway, a porter saw her pushed into the car and called the police, but he didn't remember the license plate. They didn't have anything to work on until Megan's parents got the call."

"Any demands yet?"

"The caller said she'd be returned safely when they have me. I'm to go to Devil's Lake alone. A meeting is set for tomorrow evening. If there's any hint that I have company or I'm being followed, she's dead."

His words hung in the silence, sickening him. Rage tightened its screw and he had to stand to pace. Megan had had to pay over and over again for his sins. This time, he might not be able to save her.

Might not. Who was he kidding? He didn't have a chance in hell of saving her. They had let Maria Mercer go because of the reason they had held her. They operated here in Miami. If they were seen not to keep promises, the next time they tried to put that kind of pressure on a cop, he wouldn't play along. They'd been damned careful not to let Maria see faces; grabbing her had been easy, and they'd basically thrown her in a room and locked the door, except for meals and the phone calls. Her jailer had been masked, Maria said. Or else she was just too afraid to identify him. Mac wouldn't blame her.

But Saldivar had good reason not to release Megan. She was a threat alive; dead, she couldn't open her mouth. If she and Mac both died, nobody could prove Saldivar was behind it. Besides, Megan had made the mistake of interfering in a death dear to Julio Saldivar's heart. He wouldn't appreciate that, however good intentioned she'd been.

No, she would die either way. But she wouldn't die alone. He owed her. He would have made the attempt to save her even if he didn't love her.

As it was, he didn't want to live if she didn't.

He hoped Megan knew that. He hoped she knew that he would come, that he'd do his damndest to pull off a miracle.

And he hoped she knew he would have to take the biggest gamble of his life, with *her* life on the line.

The sun was still high in the sky when Mac steered his latest rental car through the last curves up the wooded ridge that protected Devil's Lake. It was the end of summer, but the highway was still busy. Megan had told him that life here didn't change until after Labor Day weekend.

If that one chance in a million came true, if he and Megan survived tonight, Mac wouldn't mind finding out what it was like around here in the quiet winter. Who knows, maybe the sheriff's department had an opening. Megan's brother had said the worst crime they had was an occasional boat being stolen. That would make a pleasant change.

Mac's grip on the steering wheel was tight. Too tight. He made himself uncurl his fingers, then discovered five seconds later that his knuckles had turned white again. Damn. It wasn't like him to let tension interfere with his concentration this way.

He glanced again at the rearview mirror, though no one car had stayed behind him for an unreasonable length of time. If he couldn't spot a tail, nobody watching would be able to, either.

He had been directed to go to Megan's cottage—

alone—where he would be contacted this evening. Saldivar was too smart to keep to a preannounced schedule, however. Mac expected that meet to be moved up.

He didn't expect what happened as he slowed down at the outskirts of town. A dark van hurtled out of a poorly marked side road. Mac slammed on his brakes, swearing. He'd barely reached a stop on the shoulder when his car door was yanked open.

"What the hell . . ."

He recognized the man with the scar down his right cheek who grabbed his shoulder. Antonio. "If you want to see the lady alive, get your butt out of there."

Mac let himself be pulled through the door and roughly stuffed into the backseat of the van, which took off with tires skidding on the gravel and dirt of the road's shoulder. Not thirty seconds had elapsed.

How close behind had his backup been? Would they find his empty car, and have no idea where he'd disappeared to?

When his old buddy Antonio gave one more push, knocking him painfully against the armrest, he swore again. The next thing he knew, he was looking down the short barrel of a Wesson .38 Special.

Antonio smiled. "I never did like you."

"I wasn't too crazy about you, either," Mac said. Tempting though it was, he didn't allow himself a glance backward. Antonio was looking for that kind of mistake.

Unless, of course, they already knew he'd disregarded orders to come alone. Was that the explanation for the surprise pickup? Did that mean Megan was already dead?

It was a struggle to shut his emotions off with the

cool detachment that had served him well in a dangerous career. He had made the only decision he could; the only one that gave her a prayer.

"Where's the woman?" he asked.

The driver, who Mac didn't know, glanced in the rearview mirror. "You'll see her in a minute." He, too, smiled. "But not for long."

Mac held his reflected gaze longer than the bastard liked. Cold anger glinted in the dark eyes before the driver had to pay attention to the next turn.

Mac knew Devil's Lake well enough to recognize where they were. On the lake road, maybe half a mile from Megan's cottage, but heading toward the public beach. Where were they going?

He had his answer when the van swerved into the drive of a waterfront house almost hidden by a ramshackle six-foot fence and tall trees. The place had an indefinable air that made it look deserted: the windows were dark, curtains pulled, a padlock on the closed doors of the detachable garage. A summer place, Mac guessed, used without the owners' knowledge.

When the van stopped, Antonio reached with one hand to open the sliding door. Then he gestured peremptorily with the gun. "Out."

Mac didn't argue. Another old acquaintance waited there, with an uglier weapon yet: a Beretta automatic. Mac had almost liked Rafael. Ironic if Rafael would be the one to kill him.

"Hands up!" Rafael snapped. Antonio's gun poked between Mac's shoulder blades.

Rafael gave him a shove and he half fell around the front of the van. A small knot of people waited near the front porch. With a lurch in his gut he recognized Megan, who stood white-faced between Saldivar himself and another man, her hands tied in front of her. When she saw him, she made a convulsive move toward him, but she was yanked back.

Mac ended up with his cheek ground into the porch railing. Splinters and peeling paint scoured his skin. Rough hands moved over him and divested him of the automatic he carried in his shoulder holster and the smaller weapon strapped to his ankle, as well as checking him for a wire. Then his hands were wrenched behind his back and tied with cord that bit into his wrists.

At last he was spun around to face the group who waited in a silent tableau.

Megan was frozen with terror that she struggled to transform into anger. For a moment when she first saw Mac, broad-shouldered and reassuringly solid, her heart had leaped with hope before it dropped sickeningly into despair. He had come alone, and was now as helpless as she. What she'd expected him to do, she didn't know, but *something*. Something besides walking into the trap.

She had spent the two days of captivity praying for a chance to escape, but though the men guarding her had been unfailingly polite, they hadn't been careless.

She had been taken to a farmhouse somewhere out in the green valley beyond Beaverton. One country road turned into another, and she doubted she could find the house again. An interior parlor with high ceilings and no windows had been set up for her with a cot and a recliner. Twice a day she had been allowed to go to the bathroom. The boredom was almost worse than her fear.

Early this morning Saldivar himself had arrived, greeted her courteously, and returned to the dark limousine with tinted windows that was so out of place in the dusty farmyard. Megan discovered that her captors had traded in the blue car for a van; maybe in case her kidnapping had been witnessed. She was firmly escorted to the van, where she sat in the middle seat between two men. Rafael she knew; he had brought her meals and taken her to the bathroom. The other man was far more unpleasant. Antonio, he introduced himself, with a smile that made her skin crawl.

But the one who really gave her the creeps was Julio Saldivar. For some reason she hadn't expected him to be so young, or handsome, but he was both. Perhaps thirty-five, with smooth dark hair, a smile that would have been charming had those brown eyes not remained so cold, and a slender build under the most beautiful suit Megan had ever seen. When he took her hand in his and held it, her stomach roiled.

And now he was smiling in a different way altogether as he walked toward Mac, who managed to look dangerous despite the fact that his hands were tied behind his back and he had been stripped of weapons. Compared to the other men, he was big and disreputable-looking, wearing jeans, his dark-blond hair brushing his collar and an angry scrape slashing across one cheekbone. Mac's gaze met hers for a fleeting instant that told her nothing, and then he switched his attention to Saldivar.

"Let her go now."

"Not yet." Saldivar stopped not a foot in front of Mac. Still smiling, he slammed a fist into Mac's stomach. Mac doubled up, retched, then with an angry roar flung off Antonio, who'd been gripping his upper arm. Before he could reach Saldivar, who stepped back, Rafael and Antonio had wrestled him to his knees.

"You son of a . . ." A kick from Antonio doubled him up again, but somehow he pulled himself to his feet. Rage flared in his gray eyes. "You want a reputation for not keeping promises? If she doesn't walk out of here, the whole world will know what Julio's word means."

The smile was gone now. "My word means something. It means that you *will* die. This time, I'll watch to make certain." Saldivar jerked his head. "Let's go."

A hand on her shoulder wheeled Megan around and propelled her down the sloping, overgrown lawn to a ramshackle dock that reached out into the lake. The late-afternoon sun was just above the ridge and the lake glittered with blinding shards of light. A white cabin cruiser bobbed gently at its mooring on the end of the dock. A fishing pole was clamped in each corner of the stern. Megan looked frantically over her shoulder to find Mac just behind her, staggering to maintain his balance when Antonio shoved between his shoulder blades. The sound of their footsteps was hollow on the boards of the dock, a death knell.

Prodded onto the boat first, she looked back again. Hoping for comfort? She didn't get it. Instead, for one revealing moment, Mac's face gave away the terror she knew he felt for the deep water of the lake.

And then his teeth clenched tightly and his face was impassive again.

"Sit!" Rafael snapped, and Megan sagged onto the bench on one side of the stern. He sat beside her and shoved a gun into her side. It dug deeper as the cruiser swayed under Mac and Antonio's weight.

"You! Over here," Antonio said, and pushed Mac down on the other side of the cruiser. Behind him Saldivar stepped on board. The other two men, who Megan didn't know, remained on the dock. One pulled the plank back onto the dock and tossed the lines to Saldivar. The boat drifted slowly away.

"Now." Saldivar stood above Mac. "We will no doubt encounter other boats. If you make a move or say a word, the young woman will die. Do you understand?"

Through gritted teeth Mac said, "I understand, you son of a . . ."

Saldivar casually back-handed him. "You annoy me."

"A few months ago, you were stupid enough to like me, remember?"

"No." This time the smile was eerily pleasant. "You were the stupid one. Men do not lie to Julio Saldivar."

"Actually, I kind of enjoyed it."

Another back-hand. Mac's head was rocked to one side. Blood seeped from the corner of his mouth. Desperate, Megan cried, "Please."

Saldivar raised a dark brow. "I apologize. For this scene, and for your inadvertent involvement in our quarrel. I assure you it will be over soon." He nodded at one of his men. "What are you waiting for?"

Antonio said, "Just your order, Mr. Saldivar."

"Then you have it." He strolled toward the cabin. "A beautiful evening for a cruise, don't you think?"

"Bastard," Mac muttered.

Megan drew deep breaths and looked at Mac, now stiff and silent across from her. "I'm sorry, Mac," she whispered.

He tried to smile, though the result was closer

to a grimace. "Not your fault. I'm the one who's sorry."

"Shut up!" Antonio growled.

Mac shrugged and his smile faded, leaving only the pain as he looked at her. *I love you*, he wanted to say, but common sense kept him quiet. If they knew how he felt about her, it would only be another weapon.

The engine roared to life and the cruiser moved away the dock, gathering speed as it reached deeper water. The wind whipped her unconfined hair across her face, and she looked back to see the long arcing wake they had left behind them. Other boats crisscrossed their path. Megan even recognized some. That flat red speedboat that leaped across the waves ahead was the pride and joy of a friend of Bill's; her brother had dated the girl skiing behind it. A houseboat anchored by a small rocky island belonged to Pam's boyfriend. Pam might even be on it now, if she'd switched to the day shift. What would she think if she saw Megan?

It was strange, the familiarity of her surroundings and her own sensation of invisibility. The world had somehow shrunk until she and Mac were all that was real. Everything else was just a little out of focus, like a memory she couldn't totally recall.

She turned her head and saw that Saldivar was in the cabin steering the boat. Beside him Antonio pointed ahead, and with a sick feeling of dread she realized where they were going.

It had all begun here, in this cove. The sun was half behind the ridge, a brilliant orange back-lighting to the lake that was plunging into shadow. Memory and reality became even more confused. This would be a re-creation of the crime she had prevented.

But this time, she felt sure, there would be two victims. Would they hit her on the head before they threw her in? she wondered. Shoot her? Would she have to watch Mac die first, or would they torment him by killing her first?

The sound of the engine changed, became lower, deeper, as they rounded the rocky point where she had dragged Mac out of the dark water. Antonio came out of the cabin and went to one of the fishing poles. Cursing under his breath, he fiddled with the reel and at last succeeded in letting out a line, unbaited.

"You," he said to Rafael. He jerked his head at the other pole. "Julio says to do the same. Just in case we're noticed." He laughed. "Who knows, maybe we'll catch something."

Antonio pointed the snub nose of a small black revolver at Mac's head while Rafael obediently released another line to stretch, silver and deceptively fragile, out behind them.

The other boats had been left behind, Megan realized. But for the mutter of their own engine, silence was folding around them along with the shadows of dusk. Silence that would become more profound yet, when Devil's Lake closed over her head.

Megan sat staring at the point, remembering the nightmare journey up to the road, her bleeding feet, the weight of a large man bearing her down. And all for nothing, she thought, for the first time really believing that there would be no rescue. That she *would* die here. That she might as well have given up that night.

She drew a ragged breath and tore her gaze back to Mac. He looked steadily back at her, and something in his gray eyes gave her new courage. He wasn't ready to die. Megan swallowed. Damn it, neither was she!

There must be *something* they could do. If Rafael was distracted for even a moment, she could dive overboard. Her hands were tied, but in front of her. She could stay under for nearly four minutes, and with a strong dolphin kick she would surface well away from the boat.

But that was as impossible as flying away would be. Mac couldn't swim, not well enough to save himself even if his hands hadn't been tied awkwardly behind his back. The path the cabin cruiser took kept them much farther from land than they had been that night. So if they couldn't swim to shore . . .

She might as well have walked into a wall.

There was no other option.

The engine coughed, its mutter became a faint grumble and the cruiser discernibly slowed. *Oh, God*, she thought, and swallowed to hold down the terror.

But then she heard another engine, higher pitched, and behind them a smaller boat turned into the cove, too. She could make out three men, and the fishing lines that trailed the boat. They were trolling, too, paying no attention to the big white cabin cruiser cutting a quieter path across the same cove.

Antonio swore viciously.

"We'll wait." Saldivar's voice silenced him. Megan turned her head to see him standing in the low door to the cabin. "What's the hurry? A delay . . ." He shrugged. "It won't make any difference. Our friend here will die the way he was meant to. Deep, deep in the lake."

"And Megan?" Mac asked coolly.

Saldivar held out his hands, as though to ask what

he was expected to do, and smiled. That chilling smile sent a rush of undiluted fear through Megan. The pleasure in it was evil. He wasn't just a criminal making a business decision, as Mac had tried to paint him. He was crazy, a man who looked forward to tonight's task. Somehow he knew that Mac couldn't swim, and had chosen *this* death for him, despite the fact that other ways of killing him would have been far simpler.

Evil, she thought again, and hunched her shoulders against the goosebumps that chased up her arms.

Silence returned. The rock of the boat was deceptively peaceful as they moved slowly through the water with slack lines stretching behind them. Going just a little faster, the fishermen passed some distance away, following the curve of the cove. *Don't leave!* Megan wanted to scream, but as though he read her mind, Rafael shoved the barrel of his gun into her side so hard she struggled for the next breath.

Desperately, she looked again at Mac. He looked back at her so intensely, she almost forgot the pain in her side. He wanted something of her. *But what?* Megan tensed, waiting. Fear churned in her stomach.

The other boat had turned and started back, its path bringing it closer to theirs. Was he hoping it would be enough of a distraction? But for what? Three armed men against the two of them, both with their hands bound—what possible good would it do them to try anything? And then she guessed. He was hoping *she* would have a chance to escape. He knew she could, if only Rafael would take the gun away.

Megan shook her head, and Mac frowned fiercely. Had he jerked his head toward the approaching boat?

Antonio stood beside one of the poles to maintain

the illusion. In the deepening dusk the faces of the fishermen were indistinct across the water.

The sound of a voice startled Megan. "Catch anything?" one of the men called.

"Nah," Antonio called back. "They're not biting tonight. We'll probably give up soon. You?"

"You don't want to give up." The fisherman gestured expansively. "We've caught a couple of good ones. And I'll tell you what, I got a hell of a bite back there." He waved again, toward the point. "Big son-of-a-bitch. If we have to stay here all night, I'm going to nail that one."

"Well, good luck," Antonio said. "Maybe we will stick around for a while."

His back was half turned to Mac, but one hand rested under his unzipped jacket, where she knew he wore a gun in the shoulder holster. But how likely was it that some vacationing fishermen would notice? And so what if they did? Even if later someone figured out what had happened, did she care? She wanted to live, not be avenged!

Mac hadn't turned his head even for an instant. His relentless gaze was still dark and intense on her. Megan licked dry lips and pleaded with her eyes for an answer. What did he expect her to *do*?

Or . . . Was he trying to tell her something? Were those fishermen the innocent vacationers they seemed? Her mind raced as she considered the possibility. Mac hadn't been as interested in them as he should have been. But what could *they* do? It was unlikely Saldivar would let them come any closer than they already were. Could they shoot accurately enough from a moving boat to make a rescue remotely possible?

And then the moment came when the boat was

closest to theirs. Mac hadn't even turned his head, though he must hear the engine behind him. He shifted slightly on the bench, leaned forward a fraction. She saw the tension glittering in his eyes, stretched tight in muscles that were bunched for action. Megan spared a quick glance at Antonio and Rafael, but both were watching the fishermen.

The other boat was in her line of sight, directly behind Mac. She, too, waited, *knew* something would happen.

"Hey!" one of the fishermen called. He stood precariously in the boat and gestured excitedly. "Hey, you've caught one!"

Antonio turned fully away from Mac to look at his pole.

"No, your other line," the fishermen said.

The hooks were unbaited, but Rafael stood to look anyway. For this one moment, the gun was no longer pointed at her.

Mac yelled, "Jump!"

Megan started to rise to her feet, but Rafael was already swinging back toward her. It was as though time had slowed, and though she moved as quickly as she could, her feet felt as if they were stuck in glue. In the next instant, Mac threw himself at her in a desperate tackle. His shoulder caught her in the stomach and she was flung backward over the low gunwale.

She had barely time to snatch a breath before she hit the water and then was borne down by Mac's weight.

One rational thought cut across her fear: *Mac couldn't swim.* He must be panicking with his hands still tied behind him, with the water pressing down on them.

She opened her eyes, but they were already so far beneath the surface that the light was murky. She grabbed for Mac, felt her way up his body to his hair and curled her fingers in it, then kicked to slow their descent. If Mac struggled . . .

But he didn't. He was so still, so limp . . . Could he have hit his head somehow as they fell overboard? Had Rafael had time to get a shot off?

Her own lungs were straining, and frantically she gave powerful scissor kicks, aiming for the gray light she could dimly see above. She'd lost all sense of direction. If she surfaced too close to the boat . . . But she needed a breath too desperately to do anything but fight to reach the air above.

When her head broke the surface she gasped in a breath as she rolled Mac onto her hip so that his face, too, was above the water. His chest expanded as he sucked in air, but she had no time for relief. Gunshots were popping like a Fourth of July celebration and she turned her head to see the cabin cruiser behind her, not fifty feet away. She didn't dare take time to find out whether they had been spotted, whether the shots were aimed at them.

"Take a breath!" she cried, and dove, praying that Mac's lungs could hold out as long as her own.

This time she swam away, back toward the point. She stayed just under the surface, her fingers maintaining their death grip in Mac's hair. He floated behind her, as relaxed as a child without grown-up fears. The trust he expressed without words awed her, as did his iron willpower. Any normal human being would be thrashing in terror.

Megan arched her back and took them to the surface again. When their heads bobbed up, she shook the water off and looked back. The fading sunset was beyond the two boats, which drifted well away. The men on board were dark silhouettes as they crouched, then rose to shoot. It was like a pantomine, not quite real. On the cruiser, one of the dark forms—Saldivar?—suddenly toppled backward over the gunwale. His guttural cry traveled hoarsely across the water. Gunfire still echoed, a nightmarish backdrop.

She realized that her hands had relaxed their grip and that Mac labored to tread water beside her. She could barely make out his face.

In the next instant the cabin cruiser exploded in a burst of orange fury. A clap like thunder hurt her ears, and flames leaped for the darkening sky.

"Dear Lord," Megan whispered, transfixed. Fire and burning debris rained down on the water.

"Do unto others," Mac murmured, just before a rolling wave caught him in the face and he sank.

Megan grabbed for his shirt and floated onto her back, pulling him with her. He spluttered for air and then swore.

"Relax," she said urgently. "Just float. You know how. I won't let go."

She tried to hold her head up so that she could hear, though waves from the explosion kept slapping against her face. She caught glimpses of bits of burning debris floating on the lake, and an orange glow that must be what was left of the cabin cruiser.

Surely the men in the other boat would come looking for them. She couldn't see it, but she strained to hear the sound of the engine.

"Mac? Megan?" At last a voice came across the water. "You out there?"

"Here!" she called desperately. "Over here!"

"We're on our way! Keep talking."

Mac's voice sounded raw, but he took up the shout, "We're here. We're okay."

It was almost dark now, but a lamp came on, sweeping across the water.

"Over here!" Megan yelled again, and the light reached her. A moment later, the boat pulled alongside.

"Thank God," somebody said, and hands reached over the side. They pulled Mac in first, then her. The night air had cooled, and she began to shake. She dropped to her knees in the bottom of the boat, Mac in a coughing heap beside her.

"Here, get your hands up and I'll cut you loose," the same voice said, and she held them up without once taking her gaze from Mac.

The ropes were wet, slick. It took a moment for a knife to saw through them. When they at last fell free, Megan flexed her fingers and felt blood rushing into her hands. Somebody else had cut Mac's bonds at the same time, and he swore and struggled to his knees.

"Megan?" He said her name with frantic urgency as he swung around until he saw her. Breathing hard, shivering, she couldn't look away from the emotion in his eyes. Her heart contracted at the shattering mix of love and remembered fear.

When he spoke, mundane words were belied by the potent look in his eyes. "Maybe those swim lessons weren't such a bad idea. What do you think? Got time to teach me?"

He was asking more, she knew with a burst of exhilaration; much more. "I'll make the time," she said, and found herself smiling ridiculously. "Whenever you're ready."

"I'm ready," he said, in a voice so fierce, so positive, tears stung her eyes. Mac's arms closed tightly around her and she felt him trembling. She hugged him back with all her strength, not caring that he was wet and cold, and that she was exhausted. Vaguely she was aware when one of the men draped a scratchy blanket around them. Inside the cocoon, Mac's lips found hers.

Megan kissed him back. They were alive, and there would be a future. Triumph rose like a tide in her, almost engulfing the tenderness and fear, the anguish and gratitude. But strongest of all was her love for a man who had been willing to die for her, and now was ready to live.

SHARE THE FUN . . .
SHARE YOUR NEW-FOUND TREASURE!!

You don't want to let your new books out of your sight? That's okay. Your friends can get their own. Order below.

No. 61 HOME FIELD ADVANTAGE by Janice Bartlett
Marian shows John there is more to life than just professional sports.

No. 87 ALL THROUGH THE HOUSE by Janice Bartlett
Abigail is just doing her job but Nate blocks her every move.

No. 142 LIFESAVER by Janice Bartlett
Megan had no choice but to save Mac's life but now she's in danger, too.

No. 88 MORE THAN A MEMORY by Lois Faye Dyer
Cole and Melanie both still burn from the heat of that long ago summer.

No. 89 JUST ONE KISS by Carole Dean
Michael is Nikki's guardian angel and too handsome for his own good.

No. 90 HOLD BACK THE NIGHT by Sandra Steffen
Shane is a man with a mission and ready for anything . . . except Starr.

No. 91 FIRST MATE by Susan Macias
It only takes a minute for Mac to see that Amy isn't so little anymore.

No. 92 TO LOVE AGAIN by Dana Lynn Hites
Cord thought just one kiss would be enough. But Honey proved him wrong!

No. 93 NO LIMIT TO LOVE by Kate Freiman
Lisa was called the "little boss" and Bruiser didn't like it one bit!

No. 94 SPECIAL EFFECTS by Jo Leigh
Catlin wouldn't fall for any tricks from Luke, the master of illusion.

No. 95 PURE INSTINCT by Ellen Fletcher
She tried but Amie couldn't forget Buck's strong arms and teasing lips.

No. 96 THERE IS A SEASON by Phyllis Houseman
The heat of the volcano rivaled the passion between Joshua and Beth.

No. 97 THE STILLMAN CURSE by Peggy Morse
Leandra thought revenge would be sweet. Todd had sweeter things in mind.

No. 98 BABY MAKES FIVE by Lacey Dancer
Cait could say 'no' to his business offer but not to Robert, the man.

No. 99 MOON SHOWERS by Laura Phillips
Both Sam and the historic Missouri home quickly won Hilary's heart.

No. 100 GARDEN OF FANTASY by Karen Rose Smith
If Beth wasn't careful, she'd fall into the arms of her enemy, Nash.

No. 101 HEARTSONG by Judi Lind
From the beginning, Matt knew Lainie wasn't a run-of-the-mill guest.

No. 102 SWEPT AWAY by Cay David
Sam was insufferable . . . and the most irresistible man Charlotte ever met.

No. 103 FOR THE THRILL by Janis Reams Hudson
Maggie hates cowboys, *all* cowboys! Alex has his work cut out for him.

No. 104 SWEET HARVEST by Lisa Ann Verge
Amanda never mixes business with pleasure but Garrick has other ideas.

No. 105 SARA'S FAMILY by Ann Justice
Harrison always gets his own way . . . until he meets stubborn Sara.

No. 106 TRAVELIN' MAN by Lois Faye Dyer
Josh needs a temporary bride. The ruse is over, can he let her go?

No. 107 STOLEN KISSES by Sally Falcon
In Jessie's search for Mr. Right, Trevor was definitely a wrong turn!

No. 108 IN YOUR DREAMS by Lynn Bulock
Meg's dreams become reality when Alex reappears in her peaceful life.
